Saving Myself

ANDREA BLACK

ISBN-10: 0615940269
ISBN-13: 978-0615940267 (Andrea Black LLC)

DEDICATION

To all the students who didn't think they could afford
their dreams.

ACKNOWLEDGMENTS

None of this would have been possible without the overwhelming support of my family and friends. I am incredibly thankful to Ashlee Bartow and Alex Hyde for taking the time to read and reread drafts. Without them I wouldn't have been able to flush out what was needed and what was irrelevant. I would also like to thank Kimberly Lance for letting me sit at her house for hours and work on *Saving Myself.* Without her help I never would have finished. I am forever in debt to Erica Johnson who listened to my complicated vision of a cover and made it a reality. Likewise, I need to thank Jason Black, my brother, who took Erica's drawing and polished it into perfection. Throughout this process I was surrounded by an incredible group of friends who kept my spirits up and continued to pretend to be interested every time I brought it up. Thank you to Sara Sullivan, Darcy Wood, Matia Clayton, Sarah Kuehl, Alex Furniss, and everyone else who listened to me blather on about it for hours.

I need to thank my incredible family for believing in my crazy ideas. Thank you to my brothers Jason and Aaron who pushed me to go for my dreams no matter how insane or improbable they sounded, my sisters Jen and Jess who became examples of the type of woman I wanted to be, my dad, Lee, for teaching me how to be realistic while also being open to the fantasy, and last, but certainly not least, my mother, Barbara, who read and edited my manuscript so many times I'm sure her eyes started to bleed. She is the woman who taught me everything including how to be a badass lady in a, sometimes, unfair world.

This book started out as a bet from two of my very best friends... I guess I won!

Saving Myself

CHAPTER ONE

I woke with a start. My long dark brown bangs clung to my forehead as I jolted forward in my queen sized bed. I clutched the large white down comforter to my chest and took a deep breath. Exhaling loudly, I took in the familiar sight of my room, and with a small shake threw the covers off. Reaching my hand through the darkness to turn on the lamp, I knocked over a precarious stack of hodgepodge papers and my too full water glass which tumbled and shattered on the hardwood floor.

"Shit," I said to myself not knowing whether it was about the mess I had just created, the papers that were now probably ruined… or maybe the dream that had been haunting me for the past week. I closed my eyes and pulled my legs to my chest, resting my head on my knees. I still couldn't remember the man from my dreams, but the things he had done to me I could feel throughout my whole body. I remembered the way his strong arms wrapped around my bare torso, how he memorized my body with his hands and mouth and how he had teased me bringing me close to the brink and then… I would wake up. EVERY TIME! No release. No escape. I felt like I was perpetually stuck at the top of the highest drop on a rollercoaster, unable to move forward or backward. I tried to focus on his face to remember who it was, but his features were blurred. The only thing I could see clearly were his deep green eyes watching me as I reacted to the things he was doing. Opening my eyes, I wiped my soaking wet bangs to the side as I tried to steady my breathing. I released my legs reluctantly bending to pick up the papers that were now thoroughly soaked. The first one I held was from Miller Cove Financial Services, the company that I used for my student loans, it read:

Dear Ms. Allen,

We regret to inform you that you have reached the maximum loan amount that you may withdraw. We value your business with us and would like to discuss options with you that may alleviate—

I stopped reading and rested the stack on my knees as anger bubbled through me. I thought about the options they had suggested, but the only option they had given me was to get a cosigner. I didn't have anyone to cosign a loan as substantial as this would need to be. I was supposed to be starting my junior year at Cranstone College in one month, but without the loan money I would not be able to afford it, pushing my graduation back yet again. Taking time off to deal with my difficult family, I hadn't enrolled at Cranston until I was twenty.

A soft knock at my door stole my attention as a tangled mess of caramel colored hair peeked around at me. Hailey, my former best friend and current roommate, entered the room and closed the door softly.

"Everything alright in here, Ginny?" Hailey looked down at me on the floor.

Seeing the water mess, she sat down and started using her oversized shirt to mop up some of the liquid.

"Another bad dream?" She looked at me sympathetically. I had started separating and spreading out the wet pages in my hands. I nodded and grabbed the towel that was hanging from a peg next to my desk. Laying it on the spread out wet pages I stood on it attempting to soak as much water out of them as possible.

"Wanna talk about it?" Hailey's shirt bottom was now soaked, and her eyes were pleading for me to open up to her. We hadn't been talking since the incident, mostly because that's all she had wanted to do since it happened. I couldn't take another "I'm so sorry" from Hailey, and even though the sight of her continually reminded me of the betrayal, I missed talking to her. I didn't have many friends in the city, aside from some schoolmates and my "get drunk" friends. Hailey and I had moved from our small town in Illinois to Chicago for school three years ago. She was the only one who knew everything about my past and present, and the only one who would understand what I was going through. Pushing aside the man from my dream, his green eyes still boring a hole through my mind, I picked up the damp towel and knelt down next to her.

"I got a letter from Miller Cove…" I started mopping at the floor, soaking up more with my damp towel then Hailey had with her shirt tail. "… No more student loan money, the well has finally dried up!"

"Just in time for you to fall down it." Hailey finished my thought, looking at me with her large brown eyes. "There has to be something you can do, I know you don't have a cosigner but maybe you could work something out with the school and make payments… or maybe you could ask her for some of the money back…" Hailey whispered that last part knowing it was going to upset me. It did. My eyes began to water and I shook my head. Hailey leaned in to hug me and I let her.

"Even if I could go the payments route with the school, I still don't have that money now." I cried into her shirt. It smelled like cigarettes and cheap cologne, I wrinkled my nose and pulled back.

"What if you took a semester off and worked more at the salon. When's the last time you got a raise? Maybe Tracey could work with you?" Hailey finished up wiping off the floor and held the soaking towel in her hands, the glass shards from the cup in a neat pile. She was right though, I hadn't had a raise in over a year and I was good at my job. Tracey owned a small boutique day spa in Eagle Fort Towers. I had started working there as a freshman and had quickly risen from lowly receptionist to assistant manager. It was an upscale salon that mainly served the companies in the building which unfortunately included the Miller Cove Financial Services. My mind ran over the faces of the men and women who frequented the spa wondering if one of my smiling regulars was really a devil in disguise.

"I could take another semester off. It's not ideal but it's actually the only viable option." I mulled it over in my head and decided that it wouldn't be so bad. Maybe I could work extra hours or even use the time away from school to get an internship. "Ok." I said resolved and maybe even a little optimistic, "That's the plan; it's not the end of the world." Hailey blanched. That was the same phrase I had thrown on the end of the fight we had had after the incident. I noticed and thought back to that night.

$$\$\$\$$

Tears were rolling down Hailey's face. She and I were standing in the middle of her childhood home. She was reaching out for me pleading for me to stay. Hailey kept sweeping her hair out of her face and I stood unmoving, eyes trained on the floor beneath my feet. And then I snapped.

"Stop talking! I get it you're sorry I know, but that doesn't change the fact that you just ripped my fucking heart out! I can't stand you right now! I can't even look at you I don't want to hear how sorry you are anymore. I hate you, but it's not the end of the world." And with that I walked out.

$$$

Trying not to let the remembered anger flood back into me I reached for the soaked towel and headed out of the room. Hailey followed me to the bathroom where I hung the towel and turned toward the kitchen. Looking at the clock on the microwave I realized I didn't actually have to be up for another couple of hours but I knew I would never be able to get back to sleep now.

"Want some coffee?" I asked. I would try and not bring up the past. I couldn't afford to live on my own and our landlord wouldn't let us out of our lease. Hailey and I were stuck together for another year.

"Yea," Hailey couldn't hide her grin and grabbed two large mugs from the cupboard. She prepared our coffees the same way we had drunk them for years; another reminder of how well she knew me, and of how long our friendship had lasted. The memories of our lazy mornings and all the fun we'd had flooded back into my mind as I waited for the coffee to brew. I filled my cup and added a splash to Hailey's. Turning to put the coffee pot back in its holder I noticed some half eaten coffee cake. Turning back, coffee cake in hand, I got an eyeful of naked man ass.

"Oh, god!" I whirled back toward the counter.

Naked man was completely, well… naked except for a pair of mismatched socks.

"That's her line," he said with a chuckle. "I need my shirt babe." I turned just enough to see Hailey, but not enough to see Naked Man and all his glory.

"Really, Hailey? Really?" I turned and started heading straight for my room.

"Ginny wait." Hailey was following me, and unfortunately Naked Man was following her.

"It's not…" Hailey started talking to my back, but Naked Man had caught up to her trying to retrieve his shirt.

"Ew. Why is this all wet did you pee or something?" he chuckled again and Hailey turned and ripped off the shirt.

"Get out!" she yelled at him throwing the shirt at his chest. I turned around hands up in the air, surrendering.

"Oh no, by all means, please stay. There's a fresh pot of coffee on and why don't you go ahead and free ball every piece of furniture we have." Not finished talking yet I turned on my roommate. "Is your self-esteem so low that you have to throw yourself at literally every single guy? I mean, can he even spell self-esteem? I would love to say that I thought you were better than that but you really aren't." With that I turned into my room and slammed the door. I couldn't hear what was specifically going on in the apartment but I could hear Hailey crying and yelling at Naked Man.

A few minutes passed and I could hear the door open and close. I instantly regretted what I said to Hailey. Sort of. I regretted that she was there to hear it. Usually I had those conversations with myself. I couldn't help how I now felt about my ex-best friend but I would rather pretend to be indifferent and ride out the rest of our lease. Suddenly exhausted I made a bee line for my bed. "What the...?" I felt the sting before I heard the crunch. I had forgotten to pick up the pile of broken glass on the floor and had just walked straight into it. I leaned on the bed and pulled my wounded foot up to check out the damage. There was a large cut on the pad of my foot, not deep but a good inch and a half long. Small drops of blood escaped before I grabbed a towel and pressed it to the injured area. Scrounging in my nightstand drawer I found a band aid and slapped it on. I lifted myself up onto the bed again pulling the covers around me praying that when I closed my eyes I would be greeted by the man with the green eyes. All I saw were memories of the awful incident that ripped apart a lifelong friendship with memories that not only severed ties with my family, but tarnished and shamed the only man I ever blindly loved.

CHAPTER TWO

I rubbed my eyes. I had fallen asleep and it was, thankfully, Hailey free. I stepped into the quiet living room. I assumed Hailey had left for work as I walked into the kitchen. The mugs from this morning's attempted coffee bonding session still sat on the table. I grabbed the coffee pot and drank straight from it. I showered and dressed, glad that it was Friday and I got paid. I didn't have to work until tomorrow afternoon but I needed to get my check and ask Tracey about a possible raise. My stomach rolled when I thought about that awkward conversation. Tracey was a fair boss, but she tied the purse strings at Lion and Lamb with a double knot.

I jumped in the shower and let my mind turn towards the man with the green eyes. I had never had a dream, well… a dream like the dream I had with someone I didn't know. I had had sex dreams before, but nothing as intense as this recent string with Mr. Green Eyes. None of the dreams that I had had starring celebrities, or that one time with my freshman econ teacher, had left me feeling so completely heartbroken upon waking. It was more than the frustration of waking up and not knowing who he was; it was like he took my breath away. BUT WHO WAS HE? I let the warm water cascade down my body, turning so it would relieve some of the stress that I stored in my shoulders and back. In my mind I rifled through the boys in my classes and the men that taught them... nope, no one at school. I thought about the patrons who visited the spa. Those were a little hazier in my mind but not one of them stuck out. The water started to cool and I reluctantly stepped out and ran a comb through my long dark brown hair. I didn't bother to dry it since it would dry impossibly straight. I put on a dark purple and grey dress that was professional but also showed a little bit of my peaches and cream skin. I wiggled my feet into a pair of high heeled sling backed shoes and tested out my wounded foot. There was a slight pinch but I could handle it.

I hopped on the bus and thirty minutes later I was walking through the revolving doors of Eagle Fort Towers. I spotted Tracey behind the large, dark, wood desk that was reception at Lion and Lamb Salon.

I worried my hands together as I approached the desk. If it was possible for someone to look more nervous than I felt, Tracey was the embodiment.

"Tracey. Hi, I was wondering if I could talk to you for a minute." I asked.

"Now isn't really a good time for me, Ginny."

She said motioning to the large stack of papers that I knew were payroll. I eyed the stack warily; I had already calculated everyone's totals; all Tracey had to do was hand them in to the accountant. I realized that since the papers were in fact not at the accountants then the likelihood of us getting our checks today was not good. Pushing the irritation aside I focused on my plan. I knew that Tracey would need to get the approval of the other two owners of the salon before granting me any raise, and that would take time... Time I didn't really have. "I didn't think you were coming in till later tonight?" Tracey looked at me hopefully. Why was she trying to change the subject? Maybe she thinks I'm putting in my notice. Things had started to go down a little with the late checks and impossible hours, but I loved my job and all the people who worked here.

"It won't take lo—" I paused. "Am I scheduled for tonight? I didn't think I worked again until tomorrow." Not wanting to piss her off right before I asked for a favor I began to ramble. "I can totally work tonight though if you need me. I must have gotten my schedules mixed up but no worries, not like I was planning on doing anything other than sit at home and..." Tracey was looking at me like I was a dumbass, though something else had caught my attention.

"Whoa dude, you're like four hours early. I know you're ridiculously excited but you have to wait until everyone else gets here." Robin, the salon's esthetician, rounded the corner leading from the back hall. Her blond curls bounced as she walked. Nudging me in the side, she finally stopped to peer down at the schedule on the computer. Robin and I had become instant friends at work, occasionally covering for one another with Tracey. At seeing Tracey's confused face Robin turned to look at me. "NO! no no nonononono. You are not getting out of this. You promised us a long time ago and… Stop!" *Oh Crap.* I thought. The paper cats, witches brooms, and pumpkins I had spent hours cutting out and taping all around the salon finally came into view. It was Halloween, and I had reluctantly promised Robin that I would go to a party tonight in the suburbs. She had sworn it would be "like a total rager". I scraped my top teeth against my bottom lip worrying it back and forth. It's not like I didn't want to go, because I did. It was just that Robin was more outgoing than I was. She was born and bred in this area and knew a ton of people, good and bad. I had no doubt that she would be the only person I knew at the party and that terrified me. I suddenly realized that I didn't know much about Robin. Although I considered her a friend it was definitely more of a work friend situation. Robin had promised me that she would take care of everything including a designated driver, but I found it hard to trust anyone with my life let alone some friend of a friend.

"I can literally see you thinking up ways to get out of this, so whatever plan you have mapped out in your head you can thoroughly shove up your ass. You are going. End of story."

"And on that note…" Tracey side stepped around Robin, the stack of papers in her arm. "Will you watch the desk while I run these to Ted? I don't know how long it will take me but you only have a fifteen minute wax before Sara starts her shift." Tracey locked eyes with Robin as she swept down and grabbed her purse from the floor. "And please make sure you clean up after your little get together tonight." She pointed a look at me. Robin had asked Tracey weeks before if we could use the salon as a meeting place and get ready here for the big party. Tracey had hesitated but agreed when Robin offered her five in-home facials and/or waxes free of charge. Everyone was meeting at seven, to get ready for the event according to Robin. Tracey headed for the door and I turned to follow trying to cement my plan in my head. I needed to ask her about the raise now. If I didn't I probably wouldn't see her again until Monday which would mean I probably wouldn't get my answer until the following Monday after she asked the other owners. I turned to follow her but was roughly halted by someone sticking their finger in the strap of my dress to halt me.

"We are far from done here. I have thought up way more reasons why you absolutely need to go to this party. More so than the ones you have for why you shouldn't. I also have rebuttals for your reasons... if you were wondering." Robin was smug. She crossed her legs one over the other and leaned against the desk with a *come at me bro look*. I knew there was no way I was getting out of this. I also knew that if I tried to argue my way out of it that I wouldn't catch up to Tracey before she caught a cab to the accountants.

"Fine. I'm in." I said, "I really need to catch up

to Tracey I have to ask her something really important." I turned just in time to see Tracey step into a yellow cab that sped off down the street. "Urgghhh," I yelled, "I seriously can't catch a break today."

"Don't sweat it sweets, you can ask her tomorrow at the meeting." Robin was all smiles and helpful banter now that she knew she was getting what she wanted.

"Meeting?" There wasn't a meeting scheduled tomorrow. I would have known, because I usually scheduled the meetings. Robin pulled a flyer from the printer tray and handed it to me.

Mandatory Meeting
All Lion and Lamb Salon Employees
November 1
1:oopm

I shrugged off the feeling that I had been pushed out of a conversation the managing team had had. Maybe they decided to push up performance reviews that usually happened in December. That could actually work to my benefit when it came to the raise thing. Hell maybe they already had a raise in mind for me. I suddenly didn't hate the idea of going out with Robin and her crew. If anything, the excursion would make time move faster than sitting alone in my apartment.

"Ok, so you know how you have that thing about showing off too much skin? Well I took it into consideration when I picked out your costume... you're welcome." Robin leaned over the desk smiling widely exposing her perfectly straight, perfectly white teeth. *OH GOD* I thought. When Robin had invited me to the party I had no idea costumes were involved, let alone that taking care of everything meant picking out a costume for me. I looked at my work friend, taking in her short skirt and her tank top. This wasn't going to end well. No, one thing was certain. This was going to end very, very badly.

CHAPTER THREE

Hours later I hopped into the backseat of a full size green minivan. The latex body suit I was wearing pinched as I sat on the tan leather seat. Having stayed at the salon rather than risk going home to face my roommate, I had been persuaded into being waxed, painted, and styled into my mystery character. Robin refused to show me the costume the entire time and I had only gotten hints from my makeup and hair. Heavy eyeliner, false eyelashes, and an overpowering shade of red lipstick had me certain that Robin had me going to this party as a hooker. The long wavy deep red wig didn't help to confirm or deny this thought. I had drawn the line at the full Brazilian wax Robin suggested I get. Mumbling something about how I would regret it later. One thing I apparently couldn't refuse was the baby powder bath I would get in preparation to put on my outfit. By this point three of Robin's friends had shown up to get buffed and styled to perfection. Claire was a petite blonde, April a tall brunette, and Amber who had the biggest ass I had ever seen… was a brunette. They were all going as sexy cops which pretty much solidified my fears that I was going as a hooker, like some weird joke Robin was playing on me. I could just imagine the four of them sitting around trying to think of someone stupid enough to go as their hooker. So funny. I snapped out of my paranoid day dream and stared at the full body latex monstrosity that Robin was holding in her right hand, in her left a matching bra.

"Don't freak out the bra goes under the suit." Robin said when she noticed that all the color had drained from my face. "It's just a precaution to make sure your girls," she grabbed her own breasts and squeezed them, "don't fall out." *Oh great that was reassuring*, I thought. I grabbed the bra from Robin's hand and put it on. Damn, it was snug. *There is no way my boobs are going anywhere in this thing*. Together we dragged the costume over my body pulling and tugging until the resisting latex was perfectly in place. It felt more like a second skin than a piece of clothing. The zipper was in the front and started just above my crotch. I zipped it and felt it snag right between my breasts that were nicely spaced thanks to the wonder bra. *Devil bra*, I thought. I remembered that I hated this whole experience even though the smile plastered on my face told otherwise. I pulled at the zipper but it didn't budge. "What are you doing?" Robin was laughing at me.

"The zipper is stuck, I can't get it." I was

exasperated pulling at the zipper so hard I thought it might break. I tried a different tactic, unzipping it a little and then trying to zip it up again really fast. Robin walked toward me laughing with a belt in her hand. She wrapped the belt around my waist and said.

"It's not stuck, it's zipped moron." Laughing she backed up and admired her masterpiece, taking a few moments to pull a few pieces from the wig into place. Unfazed by my shocked expression Robin bent down and slid thigh high latex boots onto each of my feet and zipped them. "Oh stop, a little cleavage never hurt anyone, plus you are practically covered everywhere else." Robin slipped some black and metallic bracelets on my wrists and a belt with multiple metallic discs around my waist. Unlike the first belt that stayed firmly on my waist this one hung low around my hips.

"My work here is done." Robin stepped back with a smile, now noticing the pallor that had become my skin tone. "My work here is not done; I'm gonna go get you a drink while you admire my handy work." Robin started to slip out of the door. Turning back she added, "And don't try to take it off. Not that you could without help." She laughed and exited the bathroom. As she closed the bathroom door I was assaulted by the full length mirror that hung behind it. I looked good. Well, *it was me, but it wasn't me*, I thought. I was hardly recognizable beneath the full red wig. The suit clung to every inch of me and the high heels of the boots elongated my already long legs. A knock at the door startled me and I flushed, embarrassed that

I had been caught ogling myself. Robin entered carrying a glass with brown liquid in it. My nose identified it as whiskey before she even handed it to me.

"I don't know about this." I said as I took the glass from Robin's hand and eyed it.

"You look fantastic!" Robin said exasperated. "You always dress so... so... nice." She said the word like it was physically painful when she thought about my wardrobe. "You have this insane body that everybody notices, and then you act all weird when anyone compliments it or suggests, heaven forbid, to do naughty, socially unacceptable things to it. Then you dress like you're Velma from Scooby Doo. " Robin grinned at me dubiously and even though I was still flushed with embarrassment I started to smile too.

"I was actually talking about the whiskey, but thank you?" we both laughed, and Robin started to pull me out into the hall.

"It's better to start with the hard stuff." Robin said as we walked down the long corridor leading into reception. Being an almost 23 year old college junior I had done my fair share of drinking, but I had never been big on liquor, leaning towards wine and beer.

"I know. Beer before liquor and all that." I took a tentative sip surprised that it was whiskey and Dr. Pepper and not whiskey and Coke. We had reached the main services room that held the chairs and bays for manicures and pedicures, where the rest of the partiers were being pampered.

"Actually it's just because we have a longer

drive to get to the party." She laughed. "At this rate you can get plastered and sober up before you even get to the bar." I knew the party was in the burbs and that was pretty much it. I had assumed it was a house party but apparently it was at a bar. That almost made me feel better being in public surrounded by other people who didn't know each other. Still nervous about not knowing anyone, I protested a little when Robin slid into her esthetics room to change leaving me to enter the party room alone. I opened the door and everyone turned to look at me. Silence and shocked stares came from the entire room. I took a minute to analyze who they all were. The three sexy cops were sitting on the long pedicure bench. There was a tall lean man sitting next to Amber who I recognized from pictures as Robin's older brother, Troy. Next to him was Bradley, Robin's longtime boyfriend, who often visited the salon, and in the corner, which had been turned into a makeshift bar, was someone I couldn't place. Moving further into the room it erupted. The girls, Bradley, and Troy started cheering and whistling as I walked further into the room. My cheeks instantly burned and I was sure the deep red lipstick now perfectly matched the staining of my cheeks. Downing the rest of my drink I tried to ignore the cheering section and headed towards the bar.

"That was… interesting," said the mystery man, who now looked vaguely familiar yet I couldn't place him. His dark brown hair was shaved close to his head and his mocha skin peeked out from his uniform.

"Yea, you're telling me... Jack please?" I refilled my glass. "So what are you?" I pointed to his uniform without really looking at it. There was no way I was going back towards the cheering section although I was pretty sure I could feel Troy's eyes burning a hole in the back of my suit.

"Eagle Fort Towers Security" he turned flashing his name tag, it read Michael. I started to pale worried that we were breaking a million building rules and he was here citing every single one of them, but then noticed Michael trying to stifle a laugh. "Sorry, I'm not here to kick you out or get you all in trouble or anything. Robin invited me. I know some of the people who work at Bingo's." He finished his explanation and then stuck out his hand. "Hi. By the way I'm Michael and you look fantastic *Natasha*." He winked at me.

"Ginny, actually" I shook his hand before Robin burst into the room dressed as a Vegas dancer complete with feather head dress.

"Come on, bitches, it's time to go!" she yelled.

$$$

Troy was driving the green van. He swerved into traffic as Robin pulled out a couple of beers and started passing them around. There weren't enough seats for everyone. The sexy cops took up the entire back bench seat, Michael and I in the middle two seats. Bradley called shotgun which left Robin sitting in the well between Michael and me. Taking a beer each, Michael and I looked at each other.

"This isn't completely illegal." He said wiggling

an eyebrow at me.

"No, not at all." I laughed, dodging to keep from getting hit in the face by Robin's larger-than-life head piece.

"Drink up, bitches. This is a booze cruise!" she yelled before promptly shot-gunning her beer.

CHAPTER FOUR

By the time the van pulled off the Dan Ryan Expressway I felt like I knew Michael pretty well. He was from Georgia and had moved to Chicago with his cousin, Matt. Michael had gotten a job at Eagle Fort Towers three years ago. I was surprised that I didn't recognize him sooner since we had been working in the same building for over two years. Between the two of us, we finished six beers on the drive and we both had started to complain about how full our bladders were. I won't say that Michael is a master of peer pressure, but I will say that he is very easy to get along with. Troy pulled the van into a spot on the street.

"We're here. We're here. We're here!" Troy sang out of the window into the crowd of clustered smokers standing outside the bar. We all unfolded out of the van, stumbling a little as we found our bearings on the rough cement. If the crowd of people didn't point out the bar, the bright neon sign hanging above the door did. The sign read "BINGOS" in large red letters and then in smaller black letters "doghouse". The bar was located in a long strip of shops that looked like they hadn't been updated since the 1940's. Michael and I started speed walking hoping to find a bathroom as soon as possible. Before we reached the crowd, I abruptly turned around and grabbed Robin's arm, unwrapping her from Bradley's body.

"Ginny! Wait. Wait!" She reached back towards Bradley who was smiling and shaking his head. He mouthed "you created her", back at Robin as he started to follow us inside.

"No time, must pee. Need help, NOW!" I linked arms with Michael still towing Robin as the group of us walked into Bingos. Michael and I parted when we reached the bathrooms just past the door as we entered. Dragging Robin into the stall we started the process that would release me from my latex prison. Finally freed I plopped down onto the seat. Not remotely embarrassed that I was a.) Peeing in front of Robin or b.) Almost completely naked.

"So, what's the deal with Michael?" I asked. It wasn't necessarily meant to be a hook up question. Although Michael was attractive I had way too much on my plate already. Adding any type of romantic engagement would be impossible, but I wasn't going to shy away from a friendship that could maybe lead somewhere. Robin started laughing so hard I thought that she might have to excuse herself to use the stall next to ours.

"Gay! Gay, gay, gay," she yelled in a Broadway type voice, like she was a member of a chorus line.

"I'm surprised you haven't seen the trail of boys he has stalking him in the lobby. I'm talking Calvin Klein models." She fanned herself with her purse and then shook her head at me. Robin helped me get back into my outfit which proved harder the second time than the first. "I really did a fantastic job with your costume. Michael should be kneeling at my feet!" she admired her handy work as we washed our hands. *What did Michael have to do with my costume?* I thought. I looked into the mirror and although I recognized the character from somewhere I couldn't place it. We moved to step out into the bar. Robin noticed my confused face. "What's wrong?"

"Nothing I just can't figure out who I am. It's on the tip of my tongue." We had now entered the bar and before I could answer Michael stepped out of the men's room. He had changed into his costume which was all black and plastered to his skin. The pants were looser but the black long sleeved shirt he wore clung to every defined ab and bicep. He carried a toy bow and arrow and drew it back pointing the tip at me.

"Hawkeye! Black Widow! Where have you been all my life? Now we can really be united!" said the guy behind the bar. Michael groaned and turned his bow toward the man. He was dressed in some sort of blue suit that I couldn't make out. He poured the contents of a shaker into two shot glasses and stepped out from behind the bar. The man had turned his shield upside down and was carrying the drinks on it in our direction. I could now see that he was dressed in a Captain America costume. The bright blue fabric clung tighter to his skin than even my latex nightmare. Sweeping my eyes down his body I noticed the easy way his muscles tightened and released as he walked. Michael and Captain America exchanged brief hugs as I tried to force myself to stop staring at them. I was frozen in my spot while I ogled Michael's friend. Before I could look away they caught me staring. Mortified I searched for Robin, but she was already back in Bradley's arms, taking a sip out of his drink as they both slowly swayed to the music. Refusing to look back at the Captain and Michael, I looked around the bar. It had a decent number of people in it. Though it was still early in the night, I had no doubt that soon the place would be packed. The walls that weren't covered by wood were painted a warm cream with photos speckled throughout the place. There was a stage opposite the entrance and the bar stretched between the two, along the wall opposite the bathrooms. My eyes found their way back to the twosome who had started walking toward me. I looked at Michael refusing to acknowledge Captain America. Michael took the two green shots from the shield and handed me one.

"To Robin," he toasted, "for squeezing your fine ass into that costume for me!" he smacked my butt hard, and then downed his shot. I could hear Captain America snickering as I tipped the glass back and let the green alcohol flow down my throat. I knew I was blushing when I handed Michael the empty glass. Nervously I acknowledged Captain America as Michael took the glasses back to the bar.

"Hi, I'm Nick." He stuck out his hand encased in a blue glove. I placed my hand in his as I looked up at his face, which was mostly obscured by the mask he was wearing. The only thing visible beyond his chiseled jaw and full mouth were his eyes...his big, deep, green eyes. My stomach warmed and this time it wasn't from the alcohol. I knew those eyes. They had been burned into my skull every night for the last week. I was still holding his strong hand in mine and my mind flashed to the things those hands might be capable of doing, or did. No, I thought confused, he didn't do those things in my dream. I had never met him before. He stared down at me and a small smile pulled at one side of his face. I realized I still hadn't released his hand and was now subconsciously rubbing my thumb back and forth across his skin.

"Ginny." I whispered and with a little shake of my head regained full use of my brain. I released his hand and scraped my teeth over my lips.

"Thanks for being our Black Widow, Ginny." He exaggerated checking out my costume. Taking his time to tear his eyes from me he said, "As you can see most of the team has assembled." Nick pointed out a man dressed as Thor in the back corner. "That's Ben." Then he pointed to two other men behind the bar. One had a red t-shirt on with a flashlight taped to it, and the other was shirtless every inch of his exposed skin painted green. "The sorry excuse for Iron Man is Bobby, and the attention whore, Hulk, is Max." Bobby was spending most of his time talking to a girl who was dressed as the Pink Ranger from Power Rangers and

27

Max had a harem of girls vying for his attention. Both men were mixing drinks. I laughed as Max tried to sweep a piece of hair behind a girl's ear and managed to wipe green paint all over her face. "Watch out for Max he's a real charmer." Nick broke out a huge smile that simultaneously caught me off guard and made my stomach drop. I wished he would take off the mask so I could get the full effect of his gorgeousness. I was positive Nick looked just as good out of his costume as he did in it. Nick and I both laughed as Max's efforts to wipe off the green paint only made it smear that much worse. "I'd better get you a drink before you kick my ass." Nick said with a smile. I followed him to the bar and leaned on the counter as Nick stepped behind it. He looked up at me waiting for me to give him my order. I was lost in his eyes again, trying to remember features of the mystery man from my dreams. I tried and failed to compare the two men currently occupying my thoughts.

"Beer, whatever's on tap, thanks." I said finally finding my voice. Nick pulled a chilled glass from somewhere beneath the bar and started to fill it. Looking around at the rest of the patrons Nick, seeming to think that Max and Bobby could handle the crowd, placed the glass on a coaster and settled against the counter.

"So give me the quick facts," Nick said giving me a small smirk. Confused, I just stared at him. "Ok, I'll start, if we are going to be a part of the same team, then we should probably get to know each other." He smiled wider and I was wondering if at night's end I would really be expected to fight crime with this group of incredibly attractive, but undeniably weird boys. "Full name is Nick Fort, I'm getting my Masters in English at UIC, and I work here." He finished. "Your turn."

"Umm, ok. Ginny Allen, almost junior at Cranstone College, and I work at Lion and Lamb Salon." I smiled and took a huge drink of my beer.

"Almost?" he cocked his head to the side.

"It's a long story," I said not wanting to ruin the night with explanations.

"Siblings?" he asked. I shook my head no, and took another drink.

"You?" I asked.

"Not really," he said. That was pretty much as close to a non-answer as you could get. I eyed him suspiciously for a second and he gave me another smile. Someone down at the bar called for him. "I'll be right back; don't move." He gave me that smile again and I knew I wasn't going anywhere. Playing with the rim of my glass I noticed a green body come into view. "Hey Natasha!" Max was standing in front of me. He grabbed my almost empty glass and refilled it.

"Thanks, Max, it's Ginny actually." I said taking a tentative sip. Max smiled, surprised that I knew his name. "Do me a favor?" he asked leaning close to my face. I wanted to ask where his harem went and why couldn't one of them participate in his favor, but I shrugged my shoulders half-heartedly. If this was my team for the night I might as well get on their good sides.

"Sure, I guess." I returned the smile that Max was beaming at me. He turned and started mixing things into a shaker. Once he was done he poured the contents into a shot glass. Three more times he did this until he had set four brightly colored shots in front of me. "Ok, so sometimes I get really bored and I try to think up different, interesting, new shots. I thought of these this morning. Try them out for me?"

"What's in them?" I picked up the first shot and eyed it. It was purple and smelled sweet. I knew not to take drinks from strangers, but what if the stranger was the bartender?

"See, the thing about shots, Ginny, is that they are usually made with alcohol." He was being sarcastic and awarded me with a smile. I tipped back the drink... not bad. "That one is called Bangarang." I took a drink of beer to cleanse my palate. One after another I took the rainbow colored shots. Each time Max would tell me what it was called. I only had one shot left and I could already feel the alcohol burning its way into my blood stream. Michael walked up behind me and noticed the empty shot glasses, Robin followed closely behind him.

"Jesus, Max, how many have you given her?" Michael swept down to look at me, laughing. Tipsy, I smiled at him, suddenly unsure if I had the balance to stand.

"I'm fine no worries, I'm just doing Max a favor." I said as Michael laughed harder. I looked to Robin who was eyeing Max suspiciously.

"She's fine, Michael. This girl has an iron stomach!" Max high fived me and handed me the last shot. It was light blue and almost see through. I couldn't help the pleased sound that escaped my lips as the smooth sweet liquid flowed past my tongue. Michael and Robin watched from a distance as Max leaned very close to me. "That one is called Ginny's eyes." Our noses were almost touching and although Max was handsome he was not my type at all. His pick up techniques weren't working for me, and I couldn't help the laugh that escaped from my throat at the same time I rolled my eyes. Max narrowed his eyes and then something behind me caught his attention. Before I could turn and look, a pair of arms were on either side of me. I started to relax when I recognized the blue fabric encasing the strong forearms.

"Dance with me?" Nick whispered in my ear. I nodded and he turned me to face him. He helped me off the chair and chauffeured me to the dance floor.

"Bye, Max," Robin said as both she and Michael followed behind. Nick pulled me into his arms and I relied more on his chest than I would have any other guy I had just met. The music was loud and although I knew Robin, Bradley, and Michael were dancing around us, I could only focus on Nick and those green eyes.

CHAPTER FIVE

I didn't open my eyes. My head was pounding so hard I thought that maybe they were doing construction outside my building. *Ouch* I thought, instinctively bringing my hand to my head. I pushed my bangs back from my face and wiped my eyes, my wig was nowhere to be seen. Opening my eyes I noticed the large dark smudges on my hands that at one point had been my eyeliner. I reached down to wipe the remnants of last night's debauchery on my pants. Except, I wasn't wearing any pants. In shock, I opened my eyes wider taking in the sun drenched tan leather, I wasn't safely in my bedroom as I thought. Oh, no, I was pantless in the back of Troy's van! Closing my eyes tightly I prayed I was hallucinating. I escaped for only a second before my pillow started to move.

"How ya feeling?" Nick asked soothingly rubbing my back. I sat bolt upright and scooted as far away on the small bench as I possibly could.

Pulling down the white button shirt as far as it would go over my legs. Nick was still dressed in his Captain America costume. He held his hands up palms facing me in an act of surrender.

"Oh God. We didn't…. you didn't… I didn't… sex?" I sputtered staring into his impossibly green eyes. He wasn't wearing his mask anymore and I noticed his sharp features, and how his long straight nose sat in between his eyes. His face was framed by thick dark blonde hair that hung just below his ears, and he nervously ran his hands through it pulling it haphazardly away from his face.

"Yea, no." he said dropping his hands to the tops of his muscular thighs. "I like my dates to be coherent when I sleep with them." He laughed to himself. "What exactly do you remember?" I was embarrassed by the question. I didn't usually drink much and now I had to try to remember a night that probably ended just as badly as today had started.

"I remember shots… I remember you asked me to dance…" Where the memory of someone safely taking me home should have been there was nothing. My mind was blank. I replayed the night over in my mind reliving the way Nick's hands gripped my hips as we moved as one to the music. The way he hummed the melody of songs he liked in my ear. The way I stood on my tip-toes and leaned in for a kiss. *No No No* I thought. I had tried to kiss Nick and worse yet he had rejected me turning his head so I grazed his cheek instead of his lips. My face flushed with embarrassment and I turned slightly away from him.

"Let me fill you in." Nick said pulling his foot to

rest on the top of his knee. "We were dancing and having a very good time, if I say so myself, and I turn around to grab our drinks and you disappear on me!" He made a mock shocked face as he pulled off his leather jacket and handed it to me. "I found you like an hour later taking more of Max's mystery shots." He paused to think. "You drink a lot," he said laughing, but it didn't go to his eyes. My face paled, I heard that as a statement and not a question. "You should probably talk to someone about that." His smile fell a little and he was distracted by an errant thought before turning towards me. He leaned in closer and looked at me like he was searching for something. My breath hitched. The part of my brain that registered the small space between us was minuscule compared to the part that wanted to punch Nick in the face.

"I DO NOT HAVE A DRINKING PROBLEM!" I growled. "In fact this is only the second…" I took a minute to think. "OK third time I've been drunk since my twenty first birthday! I'm sorry if I got a little carried away! God forbid I don't thoroughly plan one night of my life. If I offend you so much then why are you still here? Do you have some kind of hero complex? Oh hi, I'm Nick, " I said mockingly. "Don't mind my outfit which clearly indicates that I am perfection walking, but worry about coming on to me because I love rejecting drunk girls and then confusing them by being all nice when they wake up… in my lap. Oh and way to talk! Everyone was drinking last—" I was cut off.

"I wasn't." Nicks eyebrows had risen to the top of his head when I started my tirade.

"Oh forgive me. Let's all bow down to the only sober person at the party. You must have super strength when it comes to self-control, Captain America," I scoffed. "Yea right, more like Captain Pretentious Jackass." I had so much residual anger built up inside me I didn't care that I was yelling at Nick for all the world's problems, but I couldn't say anymore at that moment because he swiftly silenced me when he pulled my face up to meet his in the softest kiss. His hands were cold on my burning skin, but his lips were deliciously soft and warm. My shoulders relaxed as I kissed him back and all too soon he pulled away.

"Sorry. Wait, I'm not sorry, I've wanted to do that since the second you walked into the bar, and although I do have super human self-control when it comes to certain things, you are not one of them." His hands were still cupping my face. "To clear a few things up, I was the designated driver last night, although that's not the reason I wasn't drinking." He paused to think for a second then continued, "I don't reject all drunk girls I just refrain from becoming involved with them until they're sober, because honestly being the guy that preys on drunk girls at the party sounds a little rapey and I'm not a creeper." Nick removed his hands and let them rest on his thighs. I opened my mouth to say something. "Oh no, I'm not done yet," he turned to face me better. "I'm still here because you asked me to stay... well... forcefully asked," I was confused and it showed on my face. "It's a lot like begging," he said, "you wouldn't tell me where you lived. By the time I had taken everyone else home you had passed out and it was five a.m. So we just crashed here." He motioned to the parking lot we were sitting in. The bright red sign for Bingos was visible across the street. "Oh and thank you." Whatever response I had been working on left my mind.

"Thank you?" I asked confused.

Nick put his hand on my knee and squeezed it. "I work really hard to keep physically fit. It's nice to have it appreciated." His smile was full and bright.

"Oh," I turned to face him. "So I'm the jackass here." I returned his smile. "Could you explain one more thing to me?" I asked and Nick nodded. "Is this your doing?" I motioned at my outfit which consisted of my underwear and a white button down shirt that went halfway down my thighs.

"Well you tried to take off your costume for about thirty minutes before Michael and Robin had to step in. That's Michael's work shirt." He laughed. "He expects it laundered and pressed upon return, by the way." We both couldn't hold back our laughter. "I should probably be getting you home now." Nick said, helping me climb through the van to the front seat. He exited out of the sliding door and climbed into the driver's seat. Pulling up outside my building Nick put the car into park. His once smiling face was filled with concern. "Are you going to be alright getting in?"

Confused, I looked at him. "Yea I should be why?" Nick had stacked my costume in the empty space between our chairs.

"You just," he paused to run his fingers through his thick hair, "You REALLY didn't want to go home last night." He stressed the really part. I still didn't want to go home. I didn't want to have to face Hailey, but I knew I couldn't hide out in this van with Nick until my lease was up no matter how nice that sounded.

"It's complicated..." I paused searching for the right words to sum up my situation.

"You don't have to tell me now," he said smiling as he leaned over to kiss my cheek. "Anyway that's more of a third date conversation." I couldn't hide my smile. "Can I see your phone?" he asked. I pulled the device from my purse and started collecting my clothes while he put his number in my phone. "Text me so I have yours." I nodded and stepped out of the van. The air had cooled significantly and the wind bit at my exposed legs. Once safely inside the door I looked down at my phone. Nick had taken a picture of himself, morning hair and all. My phone beeped twice indicating it was dying. The display said it was eleven a.m. Running up the stairs two at a time, hoping Hailey had already left for work, I kept thinking about Nick. Was the timing right? Should I really care about the timing? With only an hour until I had to be at work I threw myself into the process of getting ready. I only let my mind wander towards Nick two or three times.

CHAPTER SIX

I immediately spotted Michael when I walked into the building later that day. He looked more like a secret service agent with his sunglasses on than someone in building security. We waved at each other and even though I didn't wear a watch I pointed at my wrist indicating I didn't have time. He nodded in understanding and mouthed the word "later". Looking into the glass windows I could see that most of the staff were already assembled in reception. I pushed open the door and went to the desk to check the schedule. I was supposed to work until close. Confused I looked around at the employees, Robin walked in and made a beeline for me.

"Do you know why all the appointments are gone?" I asked.

"What?" Robin screeched. "I had like six vag waxes today!" she turned toward the door Tracy had just emerged from.

"Everyone, if you could all follow me back," she said leading the way into the room. Robin, I, and the rest of the crew trickled in. "Feel free to help yourselves to snacks." I grabbed a drink and sat next to Robin while everyone else settled. "As you all know we have been having some financial issues with the salon. I, along with the rest of the owners, have been trying to find a way to alleviate some of the debt. Unfortunately the amount of business we take in isn't enough to cover our expenses." Tracey paused letting what she had just said sink in. I had started to shake and I felt like I was going to vomit. I could feel the tears coming to my eyes and looked at Tracey begging her not to say what I knew was coming next. "We've exhausted all of our options and I'm afraid we have no choice but to close." There it was, the bomb to blow a giant hole in my life! My stomach fell to the floor. Tracey continued to talk but I was no longer listening. My former employees were outraged and sad. They asked questions and tried to think of other options that the owners might not have thought of. I snapped out of my haze upon hearing my name.

"Of course we will give glowing recommendations to everyone. Ginny, we will need your help with that." I stood and Tracey stared at me waiting for me to say something. I was angry, sad and confused, not to mention I felt completely hopeless. Everyone was staring at me now. "How about we take a little breather and then maybe we could meet individually to discuss options." Tracey said walking over to me. "I know this is a shock, I'm sorry I couldn't tell you yesterday." I was beyond furious and cut Tracey off before she had a chance to finish.

"How long?" I was biting my lip so hard I was sure it would start to bleed soon.

"One more week open for customers, and one more week for the technicians, therapists, and estheticians. Then we have an additional week for clean out. We would really like for you to stay the full two weeks." I knew it wasn't Tracey's fault. This kind of thing happened all the time, but Tracey also had other projects. Tracey didn't rely on the salon for the majority of her income. I did.

"I need to go." I said, eyes watering. I couldn't stop the few tears that escaped.

"I understand. Call me tonight." Tracey said as I left the salon. I rounded the corner not knowing where to go. Inside or outside? Inside I thought, walking through the lobby head down. I bumped into a man in a very nice suit his hard body hitting me like a rock. Mumbling an apology I continued down through the lobby and through a corridor that led to one room I knew would be people free for at least a couple more hours. A large green door came into view and I glanced at the sign that read TRASH in big black letters. Swiping my key card I entered. No one was in there. I slid behind two wheeled dumpsters and succumbed to the gut wrenching sob that I had been holding back.

Forty minutes later, having cried myself dry, I heard someone enter. The dumpster to my right was pushed out of the way and Michael was staring down at me.

"Oh, baby," he said sympathetically sitting down

next to me and cradling me to his chest. The flood gates opened once again. "What happened?" he asked.

"They are closing the salon. I officially will be jobless in two weeks." I said. "I'm beyond screwed."

"You'll find another job." Michael said rubbing my back.

"No, Michael, I honestly don't know what I'm going to do. I'm such an idiot! I actually thought they were going to give me a raise today!" I said fresh tears springing to my eyes.

"You'll find a new job, I'll help you. It'll be alright." He said rubbing my back as I cried.

"It won't but thanks." I wiped my eyes not caring if I smeared makeup all over my face. "I can't finish school without money, I can't live in my apartment without money and I'm not qualified for anything. Oh God, I can't take off another semester! After June I'll have to start paying back my student loans!" I cried harder into Michael's chest. He tried to console me but I was starting to make myself hyperventilate. His shirt was soaked when he pulled away from me.

"There is one job," Michael said meeting my hopeful eyes. "How desperate are you?"

$$$

Michael had given me Matt's email address. Matt was Michael's cousin, and according to Michael had a number of businesses. Before handing over the scrap of paper holding the email,

Michael stressed that not all of Matt's jobs were legal, but he had mentioned needing an assistant at one point. I understood Michael's concerns but I wasn't really in a position to be picky. If I didn't find a job soon I wouldn't be able to pay rent and I had nowhere to go. I only had enough saved up for two months of rent. I updated my resume and sent it to Matt. Then I leaned back in my desk chair trying to think of something to do. *Maybe I could clean*, I thought. My room was clutter free. My large queen-sized bed was pushed up against the far wall. My desk was across from it and on the other free wall I had a small loveseat. Straightening some papers on my desk I thought about what kind of jobs Matt could be involved in. What if he was some sort of drug dealer... oh God, what if I was supposed to fill little baggies with cocaine? Could I do that? I would need a funnel. Would I have to bring my own funnel? The laptop sitting on my desk beeped indicating that I had a new email. That was fast I thought, seeing Matt's name in my inbox.

Hello Genevieve,

Thank you for your interest in the assistant position. Michael speaks highly of you. Would you be able to meet tomorrow morning around ten?
Regards,
Matt Tyler

I was bouncing up and down in my chair. Maybe

everything would work out after all. If I could land this job with Matt I would be out of danger, at least for a little while.

Hello Matt,

Yes tomorrow at ten is perfect for me.

Thank you,
Genevieve Allen

I pushed send and crossed my fingers.

CHAPTER SEVEN

I stood before Matt's door. I was dressed in a blue dress that went to my knees with a grey blazer to cover my bare arms. The weather continued to get colder and I hadn't bothered to grab my coat. I rubbed my hands together trying to warm them. At least they aren't sweaty I thought. Pooling all of my courage, I knocked.

"Coming!" yelled a voice through the door. I took a moment to take in the surroundings. I was in a warehouse that had been converted into apartments. I knew that Michael also lived in this building. The door opened. "Hi, you must be Ginny! Oh god, you're shaking. Come in, come in." Matt moved out of the way to let me past. Matt and Michael could have been twins. Michael was slightly taller than Matt, but they shared the same creamy mocha skin and clear hazel eyes. I walked into the spacious living room. A modern sectional sofa stood in the middle of the room with bookshelves covering almost every wall. A desk and computer dominated the left section of the room where a dining room table would have gone if a family lived here. Matt worked out of his home, it seemed. Matt turned and looked me over. Letting out a long whistle he said. "Michael wasn't kidding, you're a fox, Ginny! Are you sure you want to be my assistant?" Matt laughed as I squirmed uncomfortably. "I'm sorry, I'm awful I know. Have a seat." Matt motioned to the sofa and I sat. "OK, I'm going to just jump right in." he sat catty-corner to me and pulled out a printed copy of my resumé. "You are more than qualified for this position and I know you could do it with ease…" he paused, "I guess my reluctance is that I don't really know what I need or for how long I will need it. I guess figuring that out would be one of your jobs..." he laughed again. "So what are your thoughts?" I smoothed out my skirt.

"I think that I can excel at any administrative position. I'm not really sure what kind of businesses you're into, but I have a level head and a strong stomach." Matt caught the off color way that I said businesses and a small smile came into play.

"Let's just say I manage people. Sometimes we book jobs going to parties or promoting products. Other times we are promoting ourselves." He looked at me cautiously and then continued. "The schedules and paperwork for my girl−" Matt stalled "employees will probably be your biggest responsibility. I tend to jump into new projects without considering timing, so essentially you would have to handle anything that I might forget."

I was aware that some of the things Matt was saying sounded a little… well, a little off, but any job was better than no job. Plus it wasn't like Matt was asking me to do anything illegal. I would just be in charge of some filing and scheduling.

"I'm in," I said completely sure of my decision. The small part of my brain that was telling me to run was pushed into the back of my mind. I would touch on that later when I was alone, knowing that any doubt would show on my face.

"Great! Now let's decide the specifics." Matt pulled out a tablet computer and started clicking on things. He knew that I needed the job and he was also sure that I had the skill set to handle everything that he could throw at me… well maybe not everything.

$$$

One week down and one week to go.

"I'll miss you too, Sara. Seriously put me as a reference!" I yelled as I walked out the door of Lion and Lamb Salon. It was now officially closed to the public. Working both jobs was starting to wear on me, but the extra money would look so pretty in my bank account. An added bonus to working so much was that I was never at home. I'd only seen Hailey a handful of times since I started my new job with Matt.

"Wait for us!" Robin yelled, running next to Michael out of the building.

"I'm gonna be late! Hurry up!" I paused briefly and the three of us fell into stride beside each other.

"You're sure in a hurry." Robin said eyeing me. Michael pulled off his black tie and shoved it in his backpack.

"Yea, new job and all. It's kind of a bad idea to be late." I retorted.

"Sure nothing else is going on?" Robin linked arms with me, wiggling her eyebrows suggestively.

"Of course there isn't," Michael said linking arms with me on the other side. "Remember Ginny has a thing for older guys." I looked up at him as though he was insane.

"OH YEA!" Robin squealed, gaining the attention of the other people waiting for a taxi. "What was that all about on Halloween? You looked like you were about to punch that silver haired fox in the face." I dropped both of their arms as a taxi pulled up for us. We all climbed in the back seat and Michael gave his address.

"I have no idea what you're talking about. I remember dancing with Nick and then nothing." I leaned my head back against the head rest. "Wait, no I vaguely remember going to the bathroom and then nothing." I laughed, "I was a bit of a wreck. Sorry about that."

"Oh shut up." Michael said, awkwardly hugging me in the close space. "I ended up dancing on the bar in my underwear! You have nothing to apologize for."

"Ok, so you were pretty much dry humping the fuck out of Nick... how'd that go by the way?" Robin looked at me expectantly and I bit my lip to try and hide my smile.

"One story at a time!" Michael interjected.

"OK, so you were dancing and then we went to the bathroom which took forever between your latex and my feathers." Robin laughed. "I was finding feathers in places feathers don't belong! Anyway, we walked out of the bathroom and you saw this dude. I'm talking silver hair, nice suit, and a charming smile. You stomped over to him and, like, were jabbing your finger in his chest and then I went over there and pull you away from him... then we got some drinks." Robin finished her story, eyes alight with remembered excitement.

"What did I say to him?" I asked. I couldn't think of anyone I'd be that angry at besides Hailey. Well *him* too, but that was impossible. He moved to Philadelphia after the incident.

Robin shrugged, "I don't know. I walked over and I heard him say, 'I'll go, I'm leaving' and then he left."

"I don't remember that at all." I said worriedly. *No, No it couldn't be him. It was probably just someone who looked like him*, I thought.

"Anyway so tell us about you and Nick!" Michael said pulling me from my reverie.

I filled them in on the unconventional morning with Nick as we walked down the long hall leading to Matt's apartment.

"You haven't called him yet?" Michael screamed down the hall. He lived in the apartment directly across from Matt.

"I know. I will. Things have just been crazy lately," I said knowing things hadn't been so crazy that I couldn't have called him.

"Well how about you call him after work

tonight? We're having a sleepover. You have to come!" Robin said. I felt the flush taking over my face. I wanted to call Nick but I was worried I wouldn't know what to say. I wasn't exactly experienced with calling boys. I knocked on the door before pulling out the key Matt had made for me.

"Yes, on the sleepover, and maybe on the calling Nick." I pushed open the door and turned to face Robin and Michael who were ready to protest. "See you guys later," I said promptly closing the door in their shocked faces. Matt was pacing back and forth behind the couch, phone to his ear. He looked panicked.

Talking into the phone he said, "Alice, I need a favor... please! No, yes, I know, but you're on call tonight. Yes, I know it's your only night off but if you could...no I didn't know you had the kids. Could you find a babysitter?" he paused. "I literally have booked everyone else." He paused again. I took off my bag and coat and sat down at the desk that took me hours to clean yesterday. It was now covered with little pieces of paper that at one point had been a rolodex. "No don't hang up! Please this deal is huge and he expects someone to... Alice? Alice?" Matt looked at the phone. Alice had hung up. "You suck, Alice! Let's see how helpful I am when little Benji needs braces!" He yelled at the phone. I had started reorganizing the rolodex when I noticed that Matt was looking at me.

"What size dress do you wear Ginny?" Matt eyed me up and down.

"Why?" I said narrowing my eyes.

"OK, hear me out before you say no. I have a massive meeting tonight with a club owner. The goal is to have him agree to let our girls into the club every night of the week."

"To promote… things?" I interrupted, surprised that he had said they were our girls.

"Yes, to promote things." he said. "This business relationship could be the catalyst to a massive, legit, promotions business. I mean my business partner is even coming tonight, and he usually steers clear of being seen publicly with me." Matt looked frantic. He turned my computer chair to face him directly. Kneeling in front of me, he continued. "The girl I had booked to accompany me is sick and I have tried everyone else. Please save me, I can't exactly pitch a product if I don't have a sample to show." I narrowed my eyes. I didn't like the idea of being thought of as something to sell.

"I'm not just some product… I'm not even one of your girls!" I said.

"I know, but you are gorgeous, smart, funny, witty, and charming. That's all I need. If you would just dress up and come to dinner with us. Plus you'll get paid for it!" He said knowing that would peak my interest.

"I… I don't have anything to wear." I said. Matt smiled knowing I was in, he had won.

"Oh I've got you covered," he assured me.

CHAPTER EIGHT

When Matt said "he had me covered" he meant only figuratively. He had dressed me in a short red dress with a plunging neck line. The velvet dress was paired with black pumps that Matt had run out to buy while Robin had been recruited to do my makeup. When I had emerged from my makeshift dressing room, Michael and Matt cat called and whistled making me even more nervous. Robin had curled my straight hair into perfect waves. I held onto Matt's arm as we walked into a small restaurant, past the bustling tables to a back booth.

"OK, I don't really know Mr. Molvak very well but he's rich so, he's probably an asshole," Matt said, sliding in. I raised my eyebrows in surprise. I had figured that he knew this Mr. Molvak guy. Matt knew everyone... and not just their public persona...

"I am just going to talk and eat and then leave." I whispered harshly.

"That's all I need." He said. Matt squeezed my hand reassuringly as a middle aged, robust, balding man approached the table. Matt and I started to rise.

"You are gorgeous, I believe in you!" Matt whispered before loudly greeting Mr. Molvak. "Mr. Molvak! Thank you so much for coming. Let me introduce you to Ms. Allen."

Mr. Molvak didn't take his eyes off of me. His tongue darted out of his mouth to wet his lips as he grabbed my hand and brought it to his mouth for a kiss. Still holding my hand he said, "Please call me Jeremy." His voice was low and rough indicating he had spent much of his youth smoking. I took back my hand.

"You can call me Ms. Allen." I said, wiping my sweaty hands on my dress as Matt and Jeremy started to slide into their seats. Jeremy was chuckling while Matt looked worried.

"Why don't you sit by me, sweetheart," Jeremy said to me. To Matt he said, "I like 'em feisty." I looked into Matt's pleading eyes and hesitantly sat down next to Jeremy. Jeremy's grin grew wider while Matt started speaking.

"This was a great restaurant choice, Jeremy, thank you for suggesting it…" Matt was trying to fill the awkward silence, but I was zoning him out. I was acutely aware of how close Jeremy was to me. I would try to discreetly move away from him but he would just move closer. I was now at the edge of the booth and was positive that Jeremy was going to try and sit on my lap. Matt was still talking and Jeremy was trying hard to look like he was listening. In one smooth move Jeremy put his hand on my knee and was moving it farther along my bare skin. Before I could stop it his hand had traveled from my thigh up and under my dress.

"I'm sorry that my partner is running late." Matt said as I abruptly stood hitting my head on the low hanging lamp above the table.

"Sorry," I said, steadying the lamp. "I have to use the restroom." Without a backward glance I ran to the ladies room. Throwing open the door I went up to the sink and started splashing water on my face careful not to smudge my makeup too horribly. I tried to shake off the feeling of Jeremy's hand on my leg, but it didn't work. I grabbed a handful of paper towels and wet them propping one foot on the trash can and keeping one on the floor I started scrubbing at the offending area. The skin on my thigh was turning red when I heard the door open and close.

"Sorry," I said without turning to see who had entered. "I know this probably looks really strange." I laughed a little finally starting to turn. I was stopped. Jeremy pinned my arm to my side and seized my wrist. I was trapped. I couldn't think. I couldn't breathe. *Get away from him*, I thought, but before I could move my legs his other hand was between them cupping my sensitive flesh. He hummed in my ear shooting shivers up my spine before speaking in his gravelly voice.

"This is all going so fast, but that's fine by me. The quicker we get this over with the quicker I can get out of here." Jeremy said moving his right hand along my panties. Why was he doing this? I only signed up for dinner. Not... not this.

My breath was ragged as I yelled, "Get Off Of Me!" I dropped my leg from the trash can and stepped on his foot, trying with all my strength to get away. Not even phased, he caught both of my arms behind my back and pushed my face down next to the sink. I whimpered as I felt my teeth cut into my upper lip and pain radiating through my head. He stepped closer to me pushing his groin into my backside. I thrashed around, but Jeremy only tightened his hold on me. I could feel his erection, as the tears streamed down my face. I could taste blood in my mouth as he started skimming my bare legs. "Stop! Please—please—" I said lifting my head off of the sink. I tried to look at him. Maybe if he saw my face he would stop, but before I had the chance he slammed my head back down on the sink. Lights flashed before my eyes as the pain increased.

"I said I liked 'em feisty," Jeremy said snaking his hand up my butt and back and twirling it around my hair. Pulling my hair sharply back to lift my head he whispered "I wonder, do you like it rough?" Letting go of my hair he sharply shoved his hand back under my skirt.

"No, no, please, stop please!" He started to pull down my underwear. "Stop! Matt, Help!" I yelled through my uncontrollable sobs. "Someone, Help!" I screamed thrashing on the counter. Closing my eyes I tried to think of something to say or do, something that would make him stop. I didn't hear the door open and close this time. I did hear the large crash as the trash can collided with Jeremy's head. I felt Jeremy fall onto me and then he was pulled off. I stood straight and started for the door.

Before opening it I heard the second crash and turned just in time to see Jeremy's head being pulled back and slammed into the hand dryer. This time he fell to the floor. The assault wasn't over as I saw the tall man crouch down to the floor where Jeremy was conscious and bleeding from a large cut on his head.

"Get out!" the man said still staring at Jeremy. He was dressed in a nice suit. He pulled back his arm and clenched his fist. His muscles bulged and released as his fist collided with Jeremy's face. As he continued to punch Jeremy, his nicely combed-back hair fell, covering his forehead and eyes. I was frozen staring at the gruesome scene. I turned my attention from Jeremy's bloody face to look at my savior. His face was flushed and red, his hair was shaggy and dark brown, and his eyes were intense... and a very deep green. *This is him*, I thought. Jeremy started to move and the man turned to punch him in the face again. "What are you still doing here? GO!" he yelled and this time I listened. I ran out of the bathroom, past Matt and out the doors of the restaurant.

$$$

My hands wouldn't stop shaking as I tried to get the key in the lock. Matt had tried to call me four times already but I didn't know what to say to him. I had single handedly ruined a major deal for him. Did I even still have a job? The tears continued to stream down my face as I finally got the key in. Before I could unlock it, the door swung open.

Hailey stood in her pajamas rubbing her eyes.

"Oh my God, what happened?" she asked. I pushed past her and went straight to the bathroom. I looked at myself in the mirror. Dried blood clung to half of my face and neck. I had a cut just above my eyebrow where my head had hit the faucet handle and another on my lip where it had taken the brunt of the force when Jeremy slammed my head against the counter. My thigh was still raw from where I had tried to remove the feeling of his hand. On my waist and wrists, bruises were starting to form. The attack tonight was playing through my head as I ripped off the red dress and turned on the shower. The memory of Jeremy running his hand up my legs replayed in my mind. I sat in the bathtub letting the water go from scalding to freezing as I cried. A knock on the door didn't even stir me.

"Can I come in?" Hailey asked. I didn't say anything as she entered the bathroom. She pulled a wash cloth from the shelf and started wiping the blood off my face. When I was clean Hailey turned off the water and wrapped me in a towel. She bandaged my wounds and helped me get dressed. I didn't say a word; I didn't know what to say. How did my life get so messed up? I climbed into my bed as Hailey laid down beside me, wrapping her arms around me. I tried to fall asleep but every time I closed my eyes I saw Jeremy. I couldn't stop the tears as they fell. "Please, please, Ginny talk to me." Hailey pleaded. When I didn't answer she just held me tighter.

CHAPTER NINE

I woke up to a beeping coming from my cell phone, I had a message. I tried to get up but Hailey's arms were still wrapped around me. Softly prying out of her grip I padded into the bathroom. My head pounded. Faint bruises had formed on my wrists and around the cut on my lip. I picked up my phone and a message from Matt flicked on the screen

> **Please call me! I am so sorry I had no idea what kind of man Molvak was. This is all my fault please call me. – Matt**

I dialed his number.

"Oh, thank God you're alive!" Matt answered frantically. "I need to see you! We need to talk. Please don't leave me! This is all my fault, please say something!" he finished and took a level breath.

I chewed on my lip tears threatening to fall.

All I could think to say was, "I'm so sorry Matt. I ruined your meeting."

"Fuck that deal! The only reason I would go within three feet of that son of a bitch now is to beat the shit out of him. Don't worry about the deal. It doesn't matter. All that matters is you. Do you need a doctor? Should I take you? Or can I bring you food…?" Matt was clearly trying to make up for his monumental misjudgment. I had slept almost twelve hours but I was still tired. Looking at the clock I realized I was supposed to be at Matt's now, working.

"Oh my God, I'm sorry I was supposed to come in today… if I still have a job." I said not entirely sure I still did.

"Of course you still have a job! Don't even think about coming in today though. I think you've earned a break. Hell, take the whole week off!" he said, still worried that I was going to leave him. He never knew how much he needed me before he hired me. I went quiet, I didn't want to take the week off, and I couldn't afford to take the week off. Sensing the hesitation on the other line Matt said, "I think you should take some time off, but I know that might not work for you." He paused thinking about the conversation he had had with Michael prior to meeting me. "What if I brought you some work to do at home for the week and then you come back on Friday?" I nodded and then remembered I was on the phone.

"Yea, that'd be good." I said.

"Great! I'll swing by later today and drop it off."

I sat down at the kitchen table with my coffee. "Hey Matt?" I said, sensing the end of the call.

"Yea?"

"I really am sorry about the deal." I closed my eyes, pain still shooting through my head.

"Fuck the deal, Ginny. If something happened to you I couldn't forgive myself. I don't know if I can forgive myself now. Don't even think that any of this is your fault, it never even occurred to me that Molvak was a wanna-be John. I would have never asked you to come. I wouldn't have asked anyone to come until we checked him out. It's my fault." Matt finished and I could hear the sincerity in his voice.

"Thanks Matt, I'll see you in a little bit." I said not knowing what to do with the information he had just given me.

"Alright," he said "bye."

"Bye," I answered. I knew it wasn't Matt's fault. Deep down I knew it wasn't even my fault. It was just an unfortunate experience, one I would never let myself get into again. One memory stuck out from last night, the man with the unbelievably green eyes. The man who had been haunting my dreams for weeks, and finally, the man who had saved my life. Who was he? I wanted to dive deeper into my thoughts on him, but Hailey interrupted them as she strolled into the kitchen, wincing at my face.

"I thought you left," Hailey said grabbing some coffee and sitting down.

"No, I just got a reprieve from work so I've got the weekend pretty much free," I said, thinking about the work that Matt was going to bring and my last week at Lion and Lamb Salon. "I think I'll probably just veg out, catch up on TV, or sleep or something." I said staring into my coffee and avoiding her gaze.

"Are you really not going to tell me what happened last night?" she asked.

"Nothing happened. It was just a bad night, a huge," I paused, "miscommunication," I finished. No way was I going to tell Hailey what actually happened. Better to keep the two worlds separate. Hailey stood up and walked around the table, grabbing my face to get a better look at my cuts.

"Nothing happened? You come home bleeding, barely able to speak and now you say nothing happened?" Hailey yelled. I pulled my head out of her grasp, and started to stand. "Oh great now you're just going to walk away, Ginny? Just like you always do. You've barely been home this week. I really have no idea what's going on with you anymore!" I started to leave the kitchen but Hailey grabbed my arm saying, "Why won't you talk to me?" A dull ache formed in my wrist from where Hailey grabbed it, the same place Jeremy Molvak had damaged it. Anger flooded through me as I turned to face her.

"I don't talk to you because I don't have to. We're not friends anymore! I don't understand why you can't just let this go!" I motioned at the two of us. Hailey was visibly hurt. "I'm sorry," I said not meaning it as an apology for what I said, but for the situation entirely. I opened my door, Hailey still stood in the hallway. "Thanks for last night, Hailey." I said walking into my room and closing the door.

$$$

A knock on the apartment door woke me up. As I lay in bed, I heard Hailey answer it. The voices were muffled but I could hear Matt's voice ask for me... and then the screaming began. I jumped out of bed and threw open my door.

"Are you the asshole that beat the shit out of Ginny last night? Oh, you think some cheap roses and presents are going to fix it? I should call the cops and get you..." Hailey couldn't finish before I interrupted her.

"Hailey! This isn't the guy!" I yelled. Matt looked a little shell shocked. He was dressed in blue suit pants with a white button-down shirt. He had a large bouquet of red roses and a large wrapped present. "Come in, Matt, sorry about that."

"No problem." he said. I looked at Hailey who had returned to her spot in the living room.

"Do you mind if we talk in my room?" I asked. It was the furthest room from Hailey and I didn't want to be overheard. Matt gave me a weird look and then followed me.

Once I closed the door Matt dropped the box and flowers on the bed. He ran his hands over the cuts on my face, studying them. He then moved his eyes and hands to my arms tracing the faint bruises on my wrists. He stared at them for a long time before letting one angry tear fall.

"I'm gonna kill him," he said. I wiped his tear away before turning towards the presents.

"I can't accept whatever this is, Matt." I said

eyeing the boxes warily. I motioned for him to sit in the worn love seat along the wall and I sat on my bed.

"Hey now, the flowers are the 'I'm sorry I got you beaten' present. The box is all work." I winced at his words and opened the package. Inside were a bunch of manila folders, beneath those was a brand new Macbook Pro. I pulled out the box and stared at it mouth open. "Before you say no, it's for work." Matt smiled at himself. I eyed the decrepit PC sitting on my desk and hugged the laptop to my chest. "I just want—" Matt started.

"I don't want to talk about it. It's over, it happened. I want to move on." I said. Matt nodded.

"OK, then I expect you back at the loft on Friday!" he stood and I followed. "Oh, before I forget." He pulled out a large envelope from his pocket. "Your first paycheck… well I mean its cash but still." He laughed and handed me the thick envelope. *Jesus is he paying me in ones*, I thought. "Call me if you need anything." he said walking out of my room.

"I will," I said. "don't beat yourself up too much over this."

"I will," he said sadly.

He looked so ragged. He was the protector and he had failed at his job. Resigned I said, "I know you will, but don't."

CHAPTER TEN

I woke up Monday morning and dressed for work. I had spent all of the weekend working on the project Matt had given me. I was almost done putting all of the employee information into the new database. I was amazed at the expanse of his businesses. He promoted all kinds of things from clothing to liquor, but I knew the majority of Matt's income came from a darker business... one that traded cash for flesh and as I scanned the pictures of Matt's employees I couldn't help wondering if any of these girls had had a similar incident as I had with Jeremy Molvak. I heard the door open and close and was thankful that I wouldn't have to face Hailey who hadn't stopped questioning me, especially after Matt had left Saturday. A knock on the door drew my attention; *Hailey must have forgotten her keys*, I thought. I walked into the living room and pulled the door open. Only to find Nick standing before me.

Hello, this is a surprise! What are you doing here? is what I wanted to say. "You are not Hailey," is what I actually said.

"That is accurate," Nick laughed.

"What are you doing here?" I asked, "Sorry, that was rude. Come in." I moved out of his way and he came into the apartment. We stood awkwardly. Actually I stood awkwardly, while Nick looked like he'd just stepped out of a magazine. He wore a tight v-neck black t-shirt and dark blue jeans. I couldn't help comparing his gentle green eyes to the intense eyes from the man who saved me. They were so similar, but so different.

"So, usually I'm not this forward, but you didn't call and it's been over a week and I really want to take you to lunch or dinner or something and I was hoping… do you have any plans for today?" I had almost completely forgotten about Nick and now he was standing at my door asking me on a date? I tried to hide my surprise.

"Well I'm actually heading to work now." I said, wishing I didn't have to go, while simultaneously glad I did. I never really had relationships growing up. I had been too busy with school or with my dramatic family life.

"Let me drive you." Nick said taking any scrap he could get.

I hesitated before saying "Ok, let me grab my stuff." Walking into my room, I shoved my computer and the thick envelope Matt had given me into my backpack. Together we left the apartment. Nick wasn't driving the minivan. Today he was driving a dark blue Honda Civic. He opened my door for me before he climbed in the driver's seat.

"Where to?" he asked.

"Do you know where Eagle Fort Towers is?" a small smile played on his lips, but his eyes went dark.

"Yea, I know where that is," he said pulling the car out of its parking spot. Once we hit the downtown traffic Nick started driving like a maniac. The completely sane level-headed maniac you had to be to drive in this city. Still I gripped the arm rest and closed my eyes trying to respond to Nicks questions.

"So what do you study?" he asked effortlessly navigating the city streets.

"Business Management." I said. Nick glanced at me from the corner of his eye. "I know. Really exciting right?" I laughed.

"No it's very..." Nick paused trying to think of the right word. "Practical." I laughed harder and Nick joined in. "So what are you going to do with such a practical degree?"

"Get a job." I was still chuckling. "Preferably one that pays well." I turned to take in all of Nick's features. His eyes creased from laughter. I couldn't believe how easy it was to talk to him. "So what about you?" I asked "I know you're getting your Master's in English."

"Yep, this is my last year." He smiled.

"Teaching or writing?" I asked. Nick took a minute to think.

"Can I say both? I mean I would love to write full time, but if that doesn't work out, then I would still like teaching. I mean, it's not my first love, but it's in the top five." He turned to face me, as we pulled up in front of Eagle Fort Towers.

"Wow, a plan and then a backup plan! You might be even more practical than I am." We both laughed and then it grew silent. We sat staring at each other smiling when a knock on the glass startled me. I turned and saw Tracey waving through the window. I rolled it down.

"Thank God you brought muscle." Tracey said reaching her arm through the window to shake Nick's hand. Nick spoke up before I could correct her.

"Why yes she did. Hi, I'm Nick, whatever I can do to help." he said. My mouth dropped open and I turned to stare at him. "Why don't you two head on in and I'll park the car." he said trying to hide his smile.

"That would be great, Nick. I'm Tracey. If you go through the parking garage we have an open space, #1341," Tracey said retracting her hand. I laughed and got out of the car.

"I'll see you inside, Ginny." Nick yelled before rolling up the window and driving towards the parking garage. Tracey bumped me in the side as his car turned the corner.

"Well, he's attractive," she said laughing as we walked in the building. Michael waved at me from behind security.

"Hey Michael, Nick's going to be coming in, in a minute. Could you point him toward the salon?" Michael smiled and winked at me.

"Sure thing," he said wiggling his eyebrows up and down.

Tracey immediately set me to work cleaning out the back rooms. When Nick arrived she put him to work moving furniture in reception. We barely had time to speak to each other the entire time we were there. Around six o'clock Tracey called for us to meet in reception.

"Thanks for all your hard work today, guys. I have to run, but I ordered some sandwiches to say thank you." On cue the sandwich delivery guy knocked on the glass. Tracey opened the door and paid the man. Laughing I took the bag Tracey held out and all three of us walked out the door. "I will see you tomorrow, Ginny." Tracey said locking the door. "And thank you again, Nick. We might not have to come in on Friday now!" We all said goodbye and I started to head towards the parking garage, but Nick wasn't beside me. I turned looking for him.

"Come with me," Nick said standing next to the door that led into a little courtyard. I turned to follow him. We walked down the tree lined pathway to a stone bench surrounded by flowers. The sun was out which helped negate some of the cold. "I thought we could have a picnic," Nick said sitting on the bench. I sat too. I had never realized how beautiful the courtyard was. The leaves were just starting to turn and I savored what would be one of the last nice days before winter came. "What are you thinking about?" He had been staring at me.

"I was just thinking about how much I enjoy this," I said. Nick gave me one of his toothy megawatt smiles.

"Me too," he said. We sat in silence while we ate

soaking up the cool fall air and each other's company.

"Thanks for helping today," I said.

Nick laughed, "You mean thanks for crashing your clean out?" He laughed again.

"I know it's probably not the date you had in mind when you asked me to dinner," I said shyly.

"I just wanted any date with you. I'll take what I can get." He laughed again. "Don't get me wrong though, I expect more of this and I *will* take you to dinner someday." The light made his eyes shine, but he was very serious. He wanted to make no mistake when it came to telling me his intentions. Nick didn't play games, and he wanted to make me aware of that. "I better get you home. I have to be at work in an hour." He scrunched his sandwich wrapper into a small ball, tossing our trash into the bin. Holding hands we both walked into the building and down to the garage. Settling in the car we listened to the radio, holding hands on the short drive to my apartment. Nick opened my car door and walked me to the entrance and before leaving gave me a soft kiss on the lips.

"Today was perfect," he said before turning and walking back to his car. I waved as he pulled away. Leaning against the door I pulled out my cell phone. Scrolling through the names, I climbed the steps two at a time to my apartment. There was a note taped to the inside of the door from Hailey.

Hey Ginny, going out of town will be back Friday.

Hailey

I crumpled the note, took out my phone, and clicked out a message to Nick.

I loved today. – Ginny

As I was taking off my coat and throwing my backpack in my room, the ping of an incoming message was audible through the silent apartment.

What are you doing tomorrow?
– Nick

CHAPTER ELEVEN

I dressed for work Thursday morning. The week had flown by in a blur of working at Lion and Lamb while also finishing up Matt's homework. Nick didn't return to the salon the rest of the week but we did meet for dinner every night. He took me to his favorites places and when he had to work I would sometimes sit at the bar and watch him. The evolution of our goodbye kisses were growing exponentially. We had been making out for a good fifteen minutes Wednesday night in Nick's car before I forced myself to stop.

"I've still got a couple of employees to file." I said as an excuse. Nick forced his hands to rest on the top of his thighs while his head went to the headrest. "Are you ok?" I asked. Nick's eyes were closed and his once ragged breath was evening out.

"Yea sorry I just..." he opened his eyes and turned to face me, "...needed a minute." He gave me his patent smile and stepped out of the car and around to open my door.

"Tomorrow?" I asked.

"Yea, if you don't mind waiting till about nine. I have to do inventory after class," he said.

"I'll take what I can get," I said mimicking his phrase and softly kissing him.

I pushed the memory from my mind. I had stayed up later than usual finishing the workload Matt had given me. I wanted to surprise him this afternoon instead of waiting until tomorrow. I missed Matt and didn't blame him for what had happened with Molvak. We had become more like friends than coworkers and I hoped he didn't blame me.

$$$

"Ginny, thank you so much for staying on and helping clean out the salon. I know it wasn't easy for you," Tracey said hugging me tightly. We had grown to like and respect each other and I knew this was probably the last time I'd see her. "Ok, so we have a ton of product that we couldn't sell off and if you want it, it's yours." Tracey motioned to three large boxes. *That's why she wanted me to bring my car*, I thought.

"Tracey, thank you! I'm really going to miss this place," I said tearing up a little.

"Do not cry!" Tracey said handing me a box. "We still have to get these to your car." Once the boxes were loaded we said our final goodbyes. Even Tracey had tears in her eyes as we parted ways. I got into my car and started it. It was only three o'clock, too early to go to Matt's. Before

Tracey had left she slipped an envelope with my last check into my hand. Remembering I still had the cash from Matt I decided to head to the bank. Pulling up at the drive-thru I rummaged in my back pack for the envelope.

"Hello! How are you today?" the teller's voice rang through the speaker.

"Good, thank you. Could I have a deposit slip please?" I asked.

"Of course." The teller sent the tube with the deposit slip. I pulled out the envelope and opened it. There were no ones in the thick wad of money. I quickly counted it. It was about a thousand dollars more than I had figured it out to be. I wasn't stupid, I knew how to calculate my checks; I had done the payroll for Lion and Lamb for two years!

"Oh God," I said, "is this hush money?"

"Excuse me ma'am?" the teller chimed in. I shoved the grand back in the envelope and filled out the deposit ticket including the nice bonus from Tracey, but not including the extra thousand.

"Nothing!" I snapped, suddenly furious. I sent the tube back to the teller. Moments later I received my receipt and sped off toward Matt's condo. I could hear talking through Matt's door as I banged on it. Matt looked surprised and then confused when he answered.

"Ginny? I thought you weren't working till tomorrow. What's wrong?" he said. I pulled the envelope from my backpack and pushed it into his chest.

"What is this?" I said through clenched teeth. "Is this…" I paused not wanting to say what I thought it was payment for. "Is this hush money? For Molvak? Why…why?" I couldn't believe Matt would think so low of me. "Do you really think that little of me? That I would tell someone about what happened? I knew what I was getting into when I took this job and… and… I would never." Matt snapped out of his confused haze.

"Ginny, no, no, no," he started laughing. "That's your payment for going to the meeting. It's not hush money it's just how much you would get. Even if it hadn't turned into the colossal shit storm you would have still gotten a thousand." He handed me back the envelope.

"I don't think I believe you…" I said stopping myself from taking the money I desperately needed.

"Believe him," said a voice from inside the apartment. Matt ushered me in.

"Ginny, meet Alice. Alice, this is my assistant Ginny," Matt said.

Oh, Alice, the girl who was supposed to go out with Molvak, I thought.

"Hi!" Alice said jumping up to shake my hand. Alice was petite with a sharp angled blonde bob. "Sorry you had to go in my place. I knew that Molvak guy would be a dick… well not that much of a dick," she said sitting back down on the couch that Matt stood behind.

"Have a seat, Ginny, I'm just making dinner." He moved to head back into the kitchen.

"I really can't stay long. I just wanted to drop off the paperwork," I said sitting on the couch.

"So, what's it like working for Matt?" Alice asked. Confused, I looked at the girl.

"You tell me," I retorted as a small smile lit up Alice's heart shaped face.

"It's not really a boss employee relationship with us. It's more," Alice cocked her head to the side, "like he's my manager." I thought about that for a minute looking her over again. Alice definitely didn't look like what I had imagined a prostitute would look like. Instead of fishnets and a too-low top she had on blue jeans and a soft pink cashmere sweater. She looked more like a college student than a call girl. I wanted to ask Alice more about it but didn't know if I could handle her answers.

"What's wrong?" Alice asked noticing how conflicted I looked.

"Is it," I tried to straighten the complex personal question out in my head. "Are they, the johns, are they all like Molvak? I mean is it always like that?" My voice was small as I asked. Alice's face turned sympathetic and she scooted closer to me.

"Never! Never! Never!" she said. "That's why it's great to have Matt. If Molvak would have been a regular john, Matt wouldn't have asked you to go. He wouldn't have let you anywhere near him. He's really thorough when he checks out someone who wants to go on a date with one of us." I thought about all of the information I had input into the computer this last week. Information that went far beyond a normal background check. I had just assumed they had all been employees.

"Is it like that?" I asked embarrassed by my naivety.

"Like what?" Alice asked.

"Is it like going on a date?" I clarified. Alice

took a minute to think.

"Sometimes," she answered. "Sometimes they wine and dine you, and I'm talking nice restaurants." She laughed and continued, "Sometimes they want you to just be with them." She shrugged and turned back to me.

"But you always have to–" I started.

"Yes," Alice said before I could finish. "Well, no, but usually yes. I have this regular and sometimes he doesn't want to," she paused, "do it." She stressed the words. "Sometimes he just wants to sleep beside someone."

"Don't you get scared?"

Alice heard the question I was really asking. *Aren't you afraid someone will attack you like Jeremy attacked me?*

"Not if you do it right. Not that you did anything wrong. That guy is an egotistical asshole. The guide is basically to communicate with your date. You need to be really honest when it comes to what you will and will not do. You also have to trust Matt. He would never let you go with someone that didn't check out, and you check in with Matt throughout the date," she finished.

"I'll never forgive myself for Molvak," Matt said appearing from behind the wall. "I turned off that part of my brain, the part that is always looking for the bad in people and I switched on the money hungry part," he said sitting on the other side of me. "When you showed up today, I thought for sure you were coming over to quit on me."

"I just, I love working here, and I want to put Molvak in the past," I said rubbing my thumb along the edge of the envelope that held my payment for that night. "But I can't get him out of my head. It's like that night is on a continual loop."

"Tell me what I can do. I'll do anything," Matt said.

"There's nothing you can do, Matt." Alice chimed in, turning to me. "You just live with it and eventually it won't hurt so much." She was right. There was nothing anyone could do to help me. I opened and closed the envelope subconsciously.

"You are keeping that," Matt said looking at the envelope. He was crestfallen. All he ever wanted to do was protect me from everything... Little did he know that he couldn't protect me from my past which was doomed to repeat itself. The only difference was that this time I would be the villain.

"I guess I've earned it." I said sticking the money into my backpack.

$$$

Nick's lips were persistent on mine as we awkwardly walked up the steps to my apartment. He was careful not to touch the bruised areas on my body, and didn't press me when I gave him some bullshit excuse about falling. The small romantic restaurant we went to for dinner was only eclipsed by the amazing conversation we had. I felt so comfortable with Nick. Finally reaching the door I broke the kiss to turn and unlock it. Nick seized my earlobe in his lips and started sucking before trailing kisses down my neck to my collarbone. Momentarily distracted I finally managed to unlock the door. Turning back to meet his waiting mouth I kissed him deeply before leading him back into the apartment. I didn't care that we had only been going out a week I didn't care that our relationship wasn't defined. I only cared about the way Nick was making me feel right now. When I was with him I didn't think about Molvak. In his arms I felt completely safe. Suddenly Nick released me and straightened. Confused, I looked up at him but he wasn't looking at me, he was looking past me into the living room. Turning to see what he was looking at I froze.

"Hi, I'm Nick," he said trying to step around me to greet the two people sitting in my living room. I stopped him.

"Nick, I need you to leave," I said all warmth dropped from my voice. He put his hand on my arm.

"Are you sure?" he said looking back at the two sitting on the couch. "Is everything alright?"

"Yes, just please," I eyed the still open door and with a brief hesitation Nick left.

"What the fuck are you doing here?" I yelled. "Get out!" I walked further into the living room where my stepfather, Derek Bracken, and Hailey were sitting. The last time I had seen the two together was the night I caught them banging on Hailey's childhood bed.

CHAPTER TWELVE

I looked into the eyes of my would be dad. His hair had lost all of the rich brown color it had once had. His eyes lacked the familiar warmth. *Good*, I thought. He deserved to be miserable. I hope that his guilt eats him alive. There was a moment, right after he abandoned us, when I wished he had never come. I had prayed to wake up one day and run into the arms of my real dad, but I knew that probably wouldn't have ended up much better. My biological father had died in a drunk driving accident when I was two. Mom always said he was the funniest, nicest, guy, but I wouldn't exactly trust her memories from those days. After he died, mom drowned herself in liquor and self-hate, before being court ordered to go to AA meetings... that is how she met Derek, through her sponsor.

"He's my guest." Hailey said as some sort of defense. She took a few steps in front of him. "He's here to help. He can stay as long as he wants." I paced the length of the living room trying to organize my thoughts into a coherent stream.

"So what's the deal here? Are you guys getting back together? Oh God, are you getting married? Please, please do the world a favor and don't. There is enough evil on this planet. Heaven forbid you procreate!" I yelled, stopping midstride as Derek stopped my rant.

"Genevieve!" he yelled.

"It's not like that...you are so off!" Hailey interjected.

"Genevieve, do not talk about things you know nothing about!" Derek yelled. "Now calm down and we can talk this all out."

"Don't tell me what to do, you're not my dad!" I said knowing it sounded juvenile, but I didn't care. Somehow, Derek always made me feel like a child anyway.

"I raised you, god dammit! I am still your father!" he said trying and failing to stay calm.

"You stopped being my father the minute you fucked my best friend!" I turned and fled to my room. I started throwing clothes in a bag and let my mind wander back to that night. I tried to shake the image of Hailey and Derek together.

I was walking to Hailey's house from home. Mom wouldn't stop nagging me about coming home more often and visiting. I wanted to see if Hailey minded leaving early and heading back to the city. I trudged through the garden heading straight for the grossly exaggerated cartoon squirrel statue that stood guard over the spare key. The house was dark which wasn't shocking. Hailey's parents had already left for their annual vacation, and she usually holed up in her room looking at old pictures and notes from high school. I turned the knob and stepped inside, mindlessly meandering through the house like it was my own. I had spent enough time there growing up that it for more like home than my own. "Hailey? Can we leave? Mom is driving me—" I had opened her bedroom door. For a moment I couldn't stop staring at the two of them entwined. I thought that I might be dreaming or that I had tripped over the squirel statue and busted my head in the garden. That was before my brain started to connect tiny moments in my mind. Tiny moments that screamed this is what was happening behind my back. Hailey and Derreck were involved. It sounded so clinical that way. They noticed me and that's when I ran. I couldn't tell if Derreck was too much of a coward to talk to me or if he was too ashamed, either way Hailey got the brunt of my anger. She deserved it. They both deserved it.

"Ginny, Derek and I aren't getting back together. We haven't even talked since our relationship ended." Hailey said through the door.

"You mean the three year romp you had while I was taking care of my drunken mother? Who was sober for thirteen years before he left her for you? That relationship?" I said snarkly. Derek officially became my new dad when I was five. He had raised me as his own.

"This isn't about that," Derek said. "I know I've made some mistakes, but this is about stopping you from making even bigger mistakes." That confused me; I thought for sure they were getting back together.

"I'm doing perfectly fine," I said.

Hailey scoffed. "Oh yea, going out with multiple guys, coming home beat up, or drunk... sometimes not coming home at all..." Hailey said from the other side of the door. She was one to talk! Her bedroom had been a revolving door ever since I found out they were sleeping together and they broke up.

"Oh my god! Are you two trying to intervention me?" I screamed now facing the door.

"We are just worried honey. This isn't like you." Derek said.

Zipping up my bag I swung open the door.

"You stopped worrying about me the minute you left us. Do you have any idea what it was like taking care of mom after you left? She spent all the money on booze. All my college money was spent on Jack and Jameson, and then I spent all of my extra money trying to clean her up thinking that would help. At least when she was drunk she would crack a smile every now and then. Now she's pretty much catatonic and when she does say something it's bitter and cynical." Turning to look at Hailey I said, "And you. We lived together for two years and the whole time you were sleeping with my dad! You two must have laughed so hard at poor Ginny trying to fix a mess that you guys made." I moved away from the two and opened the front door.

"How about we all take a minute to calm down?" Hailey said. "When you come back we can talk about this rationally." I took a few steps out of the door and started heading for the stairs.

"I'm not leaving until we sort this out!" Derek said.

I continued down the stairs yelling up to them.

"Who said I was coming back?" I pushed out of the front door and didn't turn as I heard them yelling after. I pulled out of my parking spot and started driving. I didn't have a destination. The tears finally started to fall as I blindly navigated the city. I couldn't live there anymore. I had nowhere to go. I couldn't go to Nick. I couldn't go to mom. I had no one. I was once again on my own.

CHAPTER THIRTEEN

"Your card has been declined. Do you have another form of payment?" asked Jerry, the front desk clerk at Motor Bay Motel, my home for the last week. I looked through my purse for show, knowing I wouldn't find any large pile of money. I didn't even have two nickels to rub together. The Motor Bay Motel used to be the headquarters for Matt's elicit operations. I knew the rooms were cheap and that's why I came here after the fight with Hailey and Derek.

"I...I don't," I said, closing my purse.

"Check out is at eleven," He said flatly, handing me back my useless debit card. I had spent all of my money in one week. Being an adult was hard.

The next morning I packed my stuff and headed to my car. Matt had noticed something was wrong, but I didn't tell him the extent of it, and he didn't push the subject. I couldn't focus on much at work. I just kept wondering where I was going to be

I'm

sleeping tonight. That only led me to wonder where my life was going. Would life be this hard in six months? A year? Five years? The rest of my life?

"Hey Ginny, you can go home for the night." Matt said sneaking up behind me. It was already far past the time I would usually stay till.

"I can stay and finish this up," I said motioning to the pile of work I had fabricated for myself.

"Yea... uh, I've got a lady friend coming over..." he said rubbing his head. I smiled. Matt deserved someone special in his life.

"Ok. Should I come in tomorrow?" I asked. It was usually my day off, but I really didn't want to spend the whole day worrying about my problems.

"No, go home have some fun tonight," he said. Frowning, I collected my things and left.

$$$

I didn't have any gas to drive around, and I didn't have any money to get gas, so I went to the only place I could think of. I pulled up outside of my old apartment. The lights weren't on and I wondered if Hailey was gone or asleep. I didn't want to risk seeing her. Why was I even here?

I could hear the music thumping from the bar down the street. Hailey and I used to go there to celebrate the end of a semester. Some band of notoriety was playing tonight. Their giant bus took up half of the street, and the concert goers crowded around the door to the venue. I wish I had a nice big bus with a tv and bed to sleep in tonight. Reluctantly I crawled into my backseat. *This would have to do*, I thought. I opened my last bag of crackers, from the vending machine at the motel, and scrunched my legs under me. Using one of my sweaters as a pillow I bundled myself up in the rest of my clothes. It was a full blown Chicago winter now. I shivered trying to fight off the cold and get some sleep. I couldn't shut off my brain. *Is this how homeless people become homeless? A string of bad luck?* I thought. It would be so easy to go back to my apartment, and my old life, but I couldn't do it no matter how cold or hungry or miserable I was.

$$$

The loud banging of doors woke me. The concert was over and the crowd was trickling out into the streets. The bus was gone and the street emptied as cars left to go home. I sat up in the backseat. The lights were still off in the apartment. A couple staggered from the alley having partied too hard. I watched them head towards my car walking in zig-zags trying to catch their bearings. The man was haphazardly trying to steady his girlfriend but she stumbled and fell right in front of my car.

"Are you ok?" I asked sticking my head out of the door. I grabbed a bottle of water from the passenger seat and went to try and help. The girl was on her knees. As I bent to check on her she reared her arm back and punched me in the stomach. I stumbled, surprised, giving her boyfriend opportunity to push me to the ground.

"Get her purse!" the girl yelled as she kicked my collapsed body. He stepped over me to move to the car.

"I don't think she's got anything, Amy… looks like she's living in here," he said, throwing the few possessions I had to the ground. Amy started heading towards the car, frustrated with her partner.

"Take the stereo, take the—" I recovered and hit the girl from behind. Like hell I was going to let them take the only things I had left. It was two against one, but I had nothing left to lose. A part of me thought that if they killed me, then I could stop worrying. I almost welcomed death if it would save me from a future of living and feeling like this. Unfortunately, I was raised to fight, because when you don't fight for yourself, you are weak and I hated feeling weak. The girl heard me and turned just in time for me to hit her square in the jaw. Another punch to her face and a knee to her stomach had her splayed out on the ground. I could hear the man coming towards me. The grunts from the girl had brought his attention from the car to the fight. I was exhausted.

"Amy get up!" he said before trying to tackle me. Even winded, I easily moved out of his way. He was big and slow. I mentally thanked Derek for those self-defense classes. This should be the part where I run away, but I couldn't. My adrenaline was pumping and I let the anger I had been keeping caged out. I hurled myself at him beating my fists against his face and chest. He wasn't just big, he was rock hard; a solid wall of well-toned man.

"You're going to regret that," he said smacking my hands away like they were annoying gnats. He didn't waste time, grabbing me by my throat and lifting. I tried to pry his hands off, but I was quickly running out of air. The pain radiated through me. His eyes were cold as he watched me struggle to free myself. I felt his hand tighten as he lifted me higher. With a force greater than anything I could have mustered he threw me towards my car.

$$$

"You're going to be alright, baby," Derek said wiping the blood away from my face. There wasn't much pain so I tried to sit up. What was Derek doing here? Where was I?

"What happened?" I asked. "Where am I?" I tried to open my eyes, but the light made my head explode.

"You're home," Hailey said. *Wait, what? No, No, I'm not supposed to be here!* I thought.

The room started to spin and soon Hailey and Derek's faces morphed into a blinding light as I began to wake up.

The headlights from a car burned through me as I opened my eyes. "You okay?"a man yelled from the car. My head spun as I sat up. The muggers were gone. "Hey, are you okay?" he asked again.

"Yea I'm ok," I said standing. My voice was rough and my legs shook as I struggled to stand.

"You sure?" he asked. No I wasn't sure. My head was killing me and I felt like I might be sick.

"Yea, thanks," I said as the man drove off. My eyes adjusted to the dark. My clothes were thrown on the pavement. I gathered them into the backseat.

I took inventory on the rest of my things. Everything of value was gone. Two things total; my stereo and my wallet. I didn't know what to do. I climbed in the front seat and screamed. I began to feel the tears burning down my cheeks. Could things get any worse? The crying only made my head hurt more. I needed money now but, it was more than that. *This is the final straw!* I thought as I tried to stop my body from shaking. I was tired of feeling weak and never being able to take care of myself! I wanted the power for once. I started the car, pulling onto the deserted street. I should have stayed. I should have called the cops, but in a neighborhood like this I knew that no one would come forward with information. I took a sharp right. If only I could make the kind of money I made going out with Matt all the time. Before I knew it, I had parked in front of the large warehouse. I didn't fully realize what I was doing as I climbed the stairs two at a time. I knocked loudly, not caring that it was the middle of the night and the whole building was probably asleep. The door opened a few minutes later to reveal a sleepy Matt.

"Ginny? What..." Matt said rubbing his eyes, which grew larger as he took in my appearance. My eyeliner had smudged around my large blue eyes and my hair was still rumpled from the fight. From the way my neck felt, I knew bruises would be showing soon if they hadn't already.

"I need a favor." I said not waiting for his answer. "Actually two favors..."

"Come in, what happened?" Matt said.

"I need a place to stay the night," I said while

Matt knitted his eyebrows together in confusion. "It's a long story, but I can't go back to my apartment."

"Of course you can stay here," he paused before adding, "for the night. What's the second favor?"

"Make me one of your girls," I said.

CHAPTER FOURTEEN

I woke up on Matt's couch the next morning. He refused to talk about my second favor until we had gotten some sleep. Taking a moment to listen to the silence I figured Matt was still in bed. I went to his large modern kitchen more determined than ever to get him to say yes. Pulling various ingredients out of the fridge I started making him breakfast. The smell of bacon and coffee soon had him floating into the room.

"Good Morning!" I said, handing him a cup of coffee while he slid into a chair at the table. I also slid him a plate heaping with French toast, bacon, and fruit. Matt looked like he hadn't gotten much sleep and after taking a sip of his black coffee he finally met my eyes.

"Thank you for breakfast, but my answer is no," he said flatly. My eyes narrowed and I thought about taking my breakfast back.

"Hear me out first," I said, "I will still be your

assistant I only need enough to pay off my student loans and the next two years of school. Once those are out of the way, I'll stop! Just think of how much easier it'll be for me to book girls if I used to be one of them."

"What if there's another Molvak?" he threw at me. I was sickened by the thought of him, and disappointed that Matt would bring him up.

"I trust you. I know you wouldn't put me with someone like him," I replied. Matt still didn't look convinced. "At least let me have an interview," I pleaded. I didn't even know if they had job interviews for this kind of profession but I didn't care. If I knew what he looked for in an escort then I would have a better idea of the girl I needed to be... or pretend to be. That was my plan after all. Fake it till you make it, right? Matt looked serious but eventually a sly smile took over his face.

"Okay, if you can make it through the interview process I will give you a shot" he said, still smiling. *That sounds ominous*, I thought, but I was up for a challenge.

$$$

Matt pulled out his tablet as he sat on the couch. I had dressed up for the interview in the only outfit that wasn't ruined by the thieves, and sat facing him. Matt clicked through the pages.

"Okay, Genevieve, how many sexual partners have you had?" Matt said stone faced. My mouth fell open. Sure I had expected some colorful questions but I thought Matt might ease me into it.

He was purposefully being crass to make me feel uncomfortable so I would change my mind. Before I could answer him he continued. "Do you not want to start with that one? Need time to count? How about this question, what sexual positions do you feel comfortable doing or if you don't like that one…" he paused and pulled out a Barbie doll from under a cushion "using this doll please indicate the orifices you would feel comfortable with for penile and oral penetration." That sly smile came back to his face. "Or we can stop if you've reconsidered." His smile grew. I took a deep breath and uncrossed my arms. I smoothed out my brightly flowered dress and reached for the doll.

"Here and here," I pointed to the mouth and the area, where on a real person, would be a vagina. "It would have to be a ridiculous amount of money for here." I said pointing to the doll's butt. "I'm not really sure what positions I would be comfortable with because I haven't had relations with anyone, but I'm going to go ahead and say the regular ones." I handed the doll back to Matt who now looked shocked. "I mean I guess if you had a book or something I could learn the different positions," I finished.

"What do you mean you haven't had relations with anyone?" he asked.

"I've never had sex with anyone," I said blushing a little.

"With anyone? You're a virgin?" he asked, shocked, before his face contorted into understanding. "You're a virgin!" I nodded. "But you've done other stuff?" he asked.

"Yea, I've kissed a lot of guys," I lied. I hadn't kissed hoards of guys, but the few I had, had mentioned I was pretty decent.

"Wait, have you given anyone head before?" he asked. I shook my head no. "Hand job?" he asked. Once again I shook my head in the negative. "Holy shit, Ginny, you're like a virgin, virgin!" he yelled standing up from the couch.

"I'm a fast learner," I said feeling the job slip further away. Matt laughed and put his hands to his head.

"Ginny there is no way I could send you out there. They would eat you alive! You would be scarred for life! A virgin, wow!" He laughed again and started his torturous walk back and forth. I felt like crying. What was I thinking coming here? I needed the money sure, but it wasn't worth being made fun of for a decision I didn't even know I had made. I had always put school, work, or my family in front of dating. Standing up I noticed Matt had stopped pacing again and was looking at me.

"What? Run out of ways to make me feel like crap for being a virgin? Want to shout the word virgin at me a couple more times? I could run down to the craft store pick up some glitter and we could make sparkly virgin signs with giant arrows pointing at me," I yelled at him. Matt walked back to the couch and sat beside me.

"I have an idea. I've never done it before but I saw it in a movie once," he paused, "What if we auctioned off your virginity?"

"Like to the highest bidder?" I laughed but Matt stayed serious.

"Exactly! That way we can control the situation a little more than we could if I just throw you to the wolves. I think we could make a lot of money. I mean probably not enough to pay off your loans but a large chunk at least, and we would get way more than just a regular date." I was speechless. I never imagined that Matt would actually go for it, and my excitement from earlier receded as I realized at some point in all this I would have to actually sleep with a stranger for money.

"Let's do it," I croaked. My throat had suddenly gone dry. We stood and Matt tried to hug me, but I pushed him away. "I'm going to be sick," I said clasping my hand over my mouth and running to the bathroom.

CHAPTER FIFTEEN

"OK, so we've bought you some new clothes, makeup, and shit that makes you smell delicious. What else was on the list?" Matt asked pulling out his tablet. "We still need to get you waxed, might as well do that today so you're all fresh for your lady doctor visit," he said still walking.

"Lady Doctor visit? Why do I have to go to the gynecologist? I'm a virgin. Not like I have any STDS, unless I got them from a toilet seat... oh God, can that happen?" I looked at Matt who had started laughing.

"No‒ well‒ I don't know. That's messed up though. You have to get an STD screening anyway. Plus we need a confirmation that your hymen is still present and accounted for. Do you want to go to your regular gynecologist or do you want me to set you up with the one Alice uses?"

"I have only gotten one pap smear in my entire life and it was done by the doctor who delivered me." I said. "He retired a year ago, so I guess if I have to, you can set me up with Alice's."

"Ginny! You should be going every six months! It's just the responsible thing to do!" Matt said shocked.

"Yea kind of like selling your virginity," I laughed.

"Touché," he said walking towards the parking lot. "Let's go home, I'm exhausted. Maybe you could ask Robin to wax you tonight?"

I made a sour face. "If you insist," I replied.

$$$

"Are you ready?" Robin said pushing down the paper onto the sensitive skin below my hips.

"No!" I groaned closing my eyes and clutching the sides of Michael's dining room table.

"You're being such a baby, Ginny. Robin does this for me all the time!" Michael said. I grabbed a candle from the candelabra and threw it at him. Michael's eyes were closed and the candle hit him in the chest.

"Hey no rough..." Robin paused to rip off the wax "...housing." I screamed.

"That actually wasn't so bad," I said after a few minutes. Robin continued to finish my full Brazilian, full leg, and underarms waxing. All of us were now sitting on Michael's couch. We had decided to make a sleepover out of my waxing appointment.

"So, why the sudden waxing? Things going well with you and Nick?" Robin said. I hadn't really talked to Nick since Thursday, and having made the decision to become a call girl, I didn't know if I wanted to. We hadn't gotten to the cripplingly personal family stories yet and I could end it with him before any real damage was done. I didn't want to, but knew that it was better than the alternative.

"No, I don't know, I mean I like him, but I feel like…" I didn't know what to say. I couldn't tell Robin about my new job, and I wasn't sure that Michael knew what illegal activity Matt was doing… or did he?

"Ginny, this happens all the time with girls Nick dates. I wish I could tell you why he doesn't open up to people. He used to be an open book, sometimes too open, but now I can't get him to talk about anything. If you just give him some time I know he'll talk to you." Michael explained. I hadn't really noticed that Nick hadn't told me anything personal about him or his family. I had been too busy avoiding questions about my own. It worried me a little that Michael automatically assumed Nick was the problem.

"I don't know, I guess we'll see," I said. With Nick I could pretend that I had had a normal upbringing. I had some huge pieces of my life I was hiding before I met Nick and now the lies and deceptions continued to grow. I knew it wasn't fair to keep them from him.

I slipped out of Michael's apartment the next morning and into Matt's. I got dressed and headed to my doctor's appointment.

$$$

"How was the doctor?" Matt asked meeting me at the door. He was more excited than I had seen him in awhile.

"Imagine a woman shoving a duck bill up your penis hole," I said moving to sit on the couch.

"I think I could get into that," Matt said joining me on the couch. I threw a pillow at him. Ducking, he pulled out his tablet.

"Why are you so happy?" I asked pulling my legs underneath me.

"I have been a very busy boy this morning! Not only have I finished your webpage but I have also found you a place to live, rent free." He tapped on his tablet.

"You're finally sending me to the brothel aren't you?" I said snuggling up to him. "Isn't this nice though?"

"You know I love you, but I miss my quiet clean house, and my couch, and bringing girls home whenever I want," Matt said. I rolled my eyes. "Oh stop, it's an amazing apartment. It's actually only a couple blocks from your school and rent free until you finish your degree!"

"What? How? That's like mega rich downtown condos," I said.

"I pulled in a favor. It was actually really easy," he said looking at me.

"I don't know, Matt. I don't want you to have to give away your first born or anything," I said biting my lip.

"I didn't, trust me. Anyway we can move you in tomorrow. Now please look at your page!" Matt handed me his tablet and I looked at the sleek black page. A large photo, one of the new ones Matt had taken over the weekend, was the main focal point. In the photo I was wearing a long white dress that clung to my upper body and hips, it flowed down my long legs with a slight flare. Matt had caught the setting sun perfectly framing me in its retreating light. He had chosen to display it in black and white, below the photo was the number of the burner cell phone that Matt was using for the event.

"Wow, this looks amazing, but how will they know what it's about?" I asked handing him back the tablet.

"There's a ton of symbolism in the picture, your white dress symbolizes your virginity, the setting sun represents the end of your girlhood," he paused taking in my impressed look. "I'm just kidding, Ginny. They call and I tell them, it's as easy as that." I playfully smacked him.

"When do we launch?" I asked quietly.

"Once we get the paperwork from the good Doc." You would never suspect that Matt was a pimp just by looking at him. He was confident and had a way of making everyone, even strangers, feel like they had known each other for years.

"Matt?"

"Yea?" he stopped tapping on his tablet to look at me. I didn't know how to phrase the question in my mind. I nervously rubbed my hands together not wanting to offend him. "What is it?"

"How did you get into this?" I asked looking down at his now blank tablet.

"Don't look so worried, it's really not that

mortifying. I simply met a man who had money and friends." He said turning his attention back to the, now asleep, tablet.

"Yea, but why?" I asked. I knew there had to be something in it for him other than the money.

"I was new to Chicago. I was hustling bootlegged cd's on the street while Michael was taking classes. His mom was paying for most of our utilities because we couldn't afford anything." I looked at him with disbelief. I always saw Matt as someone who always had it together. "I'm serious, our apartment consisted of one room and two cots, not even beds!" he said looking like he was telling someone else's story. Matt was very good at hiding his emotions when he wanted to. "Michael would bring his friends over. Most of them were girls, and most of them were in serious need of cash. So we started out small at the Motel and then I was working a club one night and I met Jack. We made our little deal. End of story." I involuntarily shuddered. He was skimming over the hard times for my benefit, but I knew what it was like to not have any money. I knew what it was like to be that desperate.

Taking in my slight frame and large eyes he said, "You don't have to do this, Ginny, it's not too late to call it off."

"No, I need to," I said trying to relax my shoulders. I nuzzled into his side. "How about a low key movie night, tonight?" I asked looking up into his still worried eyes.

"Baby girl, one day you will have to figure out the difference between need and want." Matt got up and walked over to the bookshelf where he kept his movies. He pulled three out and then held them in front of me to choose. We settled onto the couch with a bowl of popcorn and some M&M's. Matt opened the bag of candy and poured it in the popcorn, before pressing play on the movie. As the opening credits lit up our features I turned to Matt.

"Thank you, I needed this," I said. Matt kissed the top of my head.

"You really are a fast learner," he whispered.

$$$

"Okay, we can run in and grab everything. We have about an hour until Hailey gets off work," I said unlocking the door of my old apartment.

"An hour to pack and move everything. Sounds fun," Matt said. "This furniture is going to take forever to move." He pointed at the large bed. "Let me call Michael, I don't know if he's at work or not."

"No, no, I think we can do it," I said rolling up my sleeves.

"Why? We can just call him. It'll take less time." Matt said pulling out his phone.

"I don't want Michael to know about anything," I paused, "I haven't told him about our arrangement and I don't know if I will. If we get him to help he will start asking questions that I don't know how to answer."

"I get it, keeping the two worlds separate." Matt shook his head a little. "Then let's hurry." We didn't talk much while we finished moving my stuff. The truck Matt had rented was full, my old room empty. I walked through the apartment picking up last minute items. The mail holder was full and I riffled through looking for my name, tons of junk mail, a letter from Derek, and a letter from Nick. I didn't have time to read it before Hailey got home so I shoved everything into a plastic bag and dropped my key on the table. Before heading out the door I stopped to scribble a goodbye note to Hailey. It didn't say much, I didn't really have much to say to her, but as I wrote out the goodbye I felt a huge weight lift off my shoulders. I walked out the familiar door and didn't look back, excited and terrified that my life had changed so drastically in the last few weeks.

$$\$$$$$

"What the fuck?" I yelled as I stepped into the foyer. My new apartment had a foyer!

"I know right? I guess they use this for like corporate out of towners to stay in, but it's all yours baby, until you graduate." Matt dropped the suitcase to the ground. The apartment had a spacious living room-dining room combo, a large bedroom with an ensuite bathroom bigger than my old apartment. There was a spare bedroom, an office, and an additional bathroom. The floor to ceiling windows gave way to a large balcony with the most beautiful view of the city. The thing that surprised the both of us was that the apartment was completely furnished.

"Okay, so where am I supposed to put my stuff?" I asked running my hand along the plush soft couch.

"No offense, but if you don't put your stuff in storage and relish in the marvelousness that is this apartment I will kill you." Matt said.

"Yea, but where am I supposed to store it?" I had no idea how much a storage facility cost, but I didn't really want to spend the money that I was saving by staying here.

"You have two parking spots why don't you just keep the truck here with all your stuff in it. Just back up the trailer against the wall so no one can steal anything," Matt suggested.

"We rented the truck, Matt. I just can't keep it forever!" I said.

"Keep it for as long as you need," Matt said back.

"I shelled out a hundred dollars for two days, I can't afford that indefinitely. Just because I live in a bad ass apartment now doesn't mean I can blow all my extra money," I replied

"I own the truck, Ginny, I never use it! Just keep it for as long as you need. It's literally been sitting there for like three years," Matt said. That floored me. Matt had made it sound like he had rented the truck from somewhere when actually it was his.

"Oh, you made me pay to borrow your truck, but I've been living with you for almost a week and you wouldn't take any cash." I laughed.

"That was different. Matty's gotta eat."

CHAPTER SIXTEEN

It's live, I thought, *it's been live for three days and Matt hasn't said anything.* I paced in my new apartment and jumped slightly when I heard my phone ring. Jumping over the couch, and not bothering to look at the caller ID, I answered.

"Hey it's Nick," he said.

"Nick! Um… hi… how are you?" I hadn't talked to him since the night at my apartment with my ex-father.

"I'm…" he paused, "…confused. You haven't called or responded to my letter. Hailey said you moved out? What the hell happened?" he asked.

"It's a really long story. The move was a long time coming. I'm sorry I haven't called, it's been a busy week." I wanted to tell him everything about Hailey and my parents, but something was stopping me.

"Yea I guess with the move and all. Where are you staying now?" he asked, the concern not as prevalent in his voice.

"Here and there. What have you been up to?" I said. I would never be able to explain the new condo to him, maybe eventually I would tell him, but there was so much more that needed to be said first.

"Not nearly as much as you." he said knowing that I hadn't really answered his question. I could hear the disappointment in his tone. "I've been working a lot and school of course; Max has a few new shots for you to try." He laughed.

"I'm not sure I've recovered from the last shots," I said laughing.

"Yea, well I've been trying to get in contact with my brother, well… half-brother." Nick said. *Wow*, I thought. Nick, like me, avoided talking about his family. I knew from Michael that he had lived with his dad in Georgia when he was in high school.

"Does he live here?" I asked.

"Yea, my family are mostly located in the—" Nick stopped when he heard the doorbell ring over the line. "Do you need to get that?" he asked.

"Yea, sorry, one minute." I said walking over wondering who it could be. I opened the door and looked out into the hall at Matt.

"We need to talk." Matt said stepping inside.

"Nick, sorry I need to go, I'll call you back." I said. Clicking off the phone, my stomach dropped as I moved to sit on the couch.

"We have some offers, but it's…" He didn't finish his thought before starting another, "I'll just explain as we go." He moved to sit next to me but changed his mind. Standing in front of me he pulled out his tablet. "OK, I've checked them all out. The first guy had the second highest bid at fourteen thousand. He's been a client of ours for a while, no incidents. I think you should pick him." Matt said.

"You said the second highest bidder. What's wrong with the first?" I asked. I instantly thought back to Jeremy Molvak. "Oh no, is it Jeremy?" I asked. Matt knelt down in front of me. "No! Come on, Ginny, like I would even consider an offer from him." he paused, "You know my business partner?"

"The silent one?" I laughed a little.

"He's the highest bidder. There is a definite conflict of interest on his part, and I really don't think you should pick him," Matt said.

"How much?" I asked. If I was going to make this decision I wanted all the information. I could handle to give up a couple hundred dollars if it helped out Matt.

"I shouldn't have even told you about him, it's really bad business on his part," Matt started again.

"Matt. How much?" I asked again. Matt ran his hands over his head and face.

"He'll pay for all of your schooling."

"Everything?" I asked shocked.

"He'll pay off your existing loans and pay for you to finish your degree. You would be bound to him for a while, Ginny. It wouldn't be just one night you'd have to see him for like two years," Matt explained.

"I'd have to sleep with him for two years?" I was still in shock and very, very confused.

"No, no the sex would be just for one night, but you'd still have to see him to deal with the financial stuff." Matt said. He looked pained and I could see the conflict on his face. He knew I needed to take this deal, but he was worried about how Jack, his business partner, would leave me afterwards.

"I can't say no to it, Matt." I said "One and done, even if it does go badly I think I'll be able to handle seeing him for payments. Hell, let's make him pay it all up front. He could put it in a scholarship or trust or something." I said trying to make Matt feel better.

Matt was battling with himself, but finally he relented. "I'll set it up." My phone pinged. Matt was busy typing on his tablet, as I read the text from Nick.

Hey I miss talking to you. Dinner Saturday? – Nick

"It's all set. Saturday at 8pm. Fair Ridge Hotel." Matt said. I hadn't realized that I had started shaking. "Are you ok? Ginny, I'm serious. It's not too late if you wanna call it off." I knew Matt's concern was genuine, but I also knew I was bringing in big business.

"No, I'm fine," I said as Matt reached for his coat preparing to leave. "Wait... will you stay here tonight?" I asked. Matt looked at the door and then back to my shaking body.

"Of course," he said settling back into the couch and turning on my oversized TV. I snuggled into his side before typing out a response to Nick.

I miss talking to you too! It would have to be an early dinner.
– Ginny

CHAPTER SEVENTEEN

"I wish you would have let me ask Robin to help." Matt said releasing one of my curls from the curling iron.

"No, she can't know. Michael can't know. Only you." I said, applying one last coat of mascara to my eyelashes.

"I think you're done. I'm hosting an event tonight at, Foxies, so if you need me between the check times, call this number." He slipped a piece of paper onto the table. With a kiss to my temple he left the apartment. My hair was curly and hung past my shoulders. My eyes popped thanks to the smoky colors of my eye shadow. I had decided to wear the same dress from the last time I went out with Matt. I pulled on a black trench coat that flared at my hips, and headed out the door. I didn't know if I could tell Matt about Nick but I definitely didn't want Nick to get hurt. The taxi pulled up in front of the restaurant. Nick was leaning against the glass and I couldn't help but smile at how flawlessly casual he looked.

"Hello beautiful," he said opening my door for me. "I could have picked you up."

"I was just running a little late so I grabbed a cab, no worries." I had picked a restaurant two blocks away from the hotel. It was a nice place and usually catered to tourists. "You hungry?" I asked, "I've always wanted to try this place."

"Yea," Nick said opening the door for me. We were seated at the back of the restaurant. Four or five other couples sat spread out around us.

"I would suggest the 2011 Estancia Pinot Noir; it would complement both of your entrees," the waiter said.

"I would love..." I started. Maybe a glass or two of wine would help with my nerves.

"No thank you, we're fine." Nick said before I could finish. The waiter looked from me to Nick a little uncomfortable. But hesitantly walked away. "Do you mind if we make this a no alcohol night?"

"Yea, that's fine," I said twisting my napkin under the table and biting my lower lip.

"It's just that I've spent the last week with my mother and she likes to toss 'em back." Nick explained. He was trying to open up to me and I froze not wanting him to stop. "She's not bad anymore, not since husband number four." He laughed. I nodded. I knew what it was like having that type of mother. For a minute I stopped worrying about what would happen after dinner and just let myself fall into Nick's story.

"Mom, well she called me and asked me to be

more a part of the family a couple weeks ago, so I've been trying. I had dinner with my brother last night," he said letting the sly smile light up his face. "It wasn't awful, I mean he's still a little stiff, but I don't know." He looked up at me. I was still, perfectly still. "Sorry that was a weird way to start off a date." He made a face and laughed.

"No I like to hear about you and your family," I said my voice barely a whisper. I didn't want him to stop talking partly because I really did care about him and partly because I was worried he would ask me about my family.

"I just," he started, "I know I'm not exactly flowing with information about myself and Michael said if I really wanted a chance with you I needed to be more…" Nick paused and took my hand over the table.

"You don't need to be anything more, I already like you and whatever we need to say to each other will come out when the time is right," I said hoping he would get my double meaning. He nodded and we switched to lighter topics as we ate our food.

"Let me drive you home," Nick said wrapping his arms around my waist outside of the restaurant.

"I have to work tonight, it's not that far from here," I said. "Call me tomorrow?"

"Yes," he said leaning in for a kiss. I welcomed the kiss at first, before my conscious decided to weigh in. My stomach felt heavy as Nick tried to deepen the kiss, I hardened my lips, and pulled away slightly.

"I'm sorry, I just," I started. "Can we take this slow?" I asked reluctantly looking him in the eye.

Nick met my stare and his concerned face melted into a smile.

"Of course," he replied pulling me back into his arms for a hug. "I'll call you." He walked backwards towards his car. I continued to watch him as he moved towards the parking lot. I then headed for the hotel.

I can't do this, I thought as I pulled the collar up on my jacket. The large sign announcing the Fair Ridge Hotel was coming into view. *It's just one night*, I argued with myself. I looked at my watch, I still had forty minutes. I pulled open the doors and walked to the front desk.

"Hello, Vivie Allen checking in," I said to the man standing behind the desk.

"Hello, Ms. Allen, thank you for choosing Fair Ridge Hotel. My name is Thomas, if you need anything just ask for me," Thomas said smiling. "I see that we already have a credit card on hold for you, if I could just see your ID." I couldn't help my shaking hands as I handed him the card. I hoped he just thought it was because it was cold outside. "Thank you," Thomas said handing back my ID. "I like the name Vivie, good choice." he said. I furrowed my brow a little. "I always got called Tommy growing up, but I like Thomas better." He handed me my room key. I was too preoccupied to fully engage in the small talk. I didn't have any funny or charming stories about my nickname. The truth being that Matt had chosen to call me Vivie when he made the website. When I asked him why, he said it was to protect my real identity. I didn't really understand, I thought Matt just liked the air of mystery in all of this crap, but I trusted him and would go along with whatever he thought was best.

"Room 1414, take the elevator to the 14th floor and turn right. Can I help you with anything else?" Thomas asked. I scooped up the room key and hastily shoved it in my pocket. I missed the first couple times because my hands were shaking so badly. Frustrated I blew the bangs out of my eyes and looked up to an expectant Thomas.

"Yes, where's the bar?"

CHAPTER EIGHTEEN

Forty minutes later I stumbled down the hall of the fourteenth floor in the Fair Ridge Hotel. On my third attempt I finally managed to unlock the door and step into the room. Those three Jack and Cokes had hit me harder than I thought they would, but I wasn't even concerned with my mental awareness right now. All I cared about was finding the mini bar. The room was dark except for one light illuminating the desk. Next to the desk I found what I was looking for. Dancing over to the tiny fridge I flung it open and grabbed a can of coke and a tiny bottle of whiskey. Closing the fridge I set them on the desk.

"Ms. Vivie I presume," said a voice in the corner. I jumped a little and turned toward the sound. A man had entered the room while I was looking through the mini bar. He was still shrouded in darkness but he was coming closer. He extended his hand once he was near enough. "I'm Jack," he said. Now visible I stared gaping at him. It was the same man from the night with Jeremy. The same man who had saved my life, and the same man who still haunted my dreams. *He's Matt's partner?* I thought.

"I, I'm…" the alcohol and the shock of seeing him again left me in a haze. "I'm going to get you a glass." I said bending to retrieve two glasses. *This changed things,* I thought pouring two glasses full of whiskey and coke. I pushed away all thoughts of what this man had done to help me. I needed to focus on the job I came here to do. The profits of which would set me up for life, well, at least for the next two years. Pooling all my courage I took a large drink and turned back toward him. "Ok, so how do you want to do this?" I asked, tripping a little as I walked toward him. Jack turned on a few more lights on illuminating the entire room. It was decorated in grays and blues. The bed and furniture were all a dark soft brown. I looked at Jack, he was still aggressively handsome with a dark blue suit and a serious look on his face. He stared at me until I felt uncomfortable and had to look away.

"Are you drunk?" Jack said.

"That doesn't matter. We are here for two things. I'm here for the sex, wait no, you're here for the sex and I am here for the money. So take off your pants," I threw my arms out, closed my eyes, and fell on the bed, "I'm ready." I opened my eyes when the room fell silent except for a small amused sigh.

"I'm not sleeping with a drunk girl," he said sitting down next to me on the bed. "Why are you drunk?" he asked.

"I'm not just some drunk girl." I leaned a little closer to him. He smelled fantastic and I noticed the small amount of stubble that lined his jaw, I wanted to scrape my nails across it. Before I had the chance he turned his head to face me. Now that he was closer I was assaulted by the true power of his green eyes. The things those eyes had seen in my dreams brought a flush to my cheeks and I started to breathe heavily. Leaning in closer to him I puckered my lips and tried to kiss him. Before I could though he was on his feet and had my hand in his.

"I think you need some air," he said helping me stand. We walked out of the room and into the hallway. Jack was dragging me behind him as he led us to the stairwell and up a flight of stairs. He opened the door and, before I knew it, we were standing on the hotel's roof. He walked me over to the ledge and I held his hand tighter. I didn't realize it but I trusted him completely. Someone else might have been worried he was going to throw them off the building, but I knew I was safe. We stood near the edge and silently looked at the beautiful city. Jack turned to look at me but I was staring into the dark sky my eyes squinted like I was searching for something. Jack let go of my hand and I turned a few times still looking into the sky.

"What are you doing?" he asked.

"I'm looking for Orion." I said, still staring into the sky. "Sometimes I can see him."

"Why are you looking for Orion?" Jack said laughing a little.

"He makes me feel safe. It's stupid, I know, but I can't find him tonight." I said resigned, looking back at Jack who now wore a very serious face.

"Do you not feel safe?" he said walking towards me.

"I don't feel like I'm in danger," I said taking his hand again. Jack squeezed my hand before letting it go. He moved to the ground and laid down. "What are you doing?" I asked.

"Maybe he'll show up once the clouds move." Jack said, pulling a flask from the breast pocket of his jacket. I laid down beside him and he handed me the container after taking a sip first himself. I drank a little, whiskey my favorite, except this whiskey tasted way better than anything I had ever had before. Undoubtedly it cost four times as much as anything I had had before. I handed him the flask and we laid in silence.

"Thanks for saving me," I said puncturing the silence while still searching the dark sky.

"I was just in the right place at the right time," he said not looking at me. He took another drink from the flask. I continued to stare at him, his shaggy dark brown hair fell around the side of his face. His eyebrows knitted together in thought before they smoothed a little and he turned to look at me. "You're welcome," he said taking my hand again. "It won't be like that," he paused thinking again. "With me, it won't ever be like that," he finished. I felt incredibly warm despite the chilly bite of the wind. My stomach started to hurt and I felt dizzy despite the fact that I was laying down. "Are you ok?" Jack asked.

"I, uh, need to go inside. I don't feel well." I said sitting up too fast. Jack steadied me as I attempted to get to my feet. Together we walked back down the stairs to our room. All the whiskey had settled at the bottom of my stomach and now it wanted out. Opening the door I stumbled into the bathroom and fell over the toilet. Violently throwing up into the bowl I began to cry. Jack rushed into the bathroom and pulled my hair away from my face. He knelt beside me until my stomach was empty. I was still crying when Jack sat down and leaned against the wall next to the toilet. When he realized I was done he handed me a bottle of water and a towel. Wiping at my face and taking a tiny sip I began to straighten.

"I'm so sorry," I said not looking at him.

"It's fine. I've thrown up after drinking less than you have," he laughed at a distant memory. I started crying harder. "Why are you crying?" he asked.

"I just have a weird feeling, like déjà vu. I just wish I didn't know the reason." Jack waited silently for me to continue. "I was four and my mom was having one of her many relapses. I grabbed her drink one night and drank the whole cup. It was some fruity drink and it tasted so good, hell anything would have tasted good, I was so thirsty. My stomach hurt and I knew I was going to be sick, but when I went to the bathroom my mom was bent over the toilet just like me." I slurred crying harder. Jack pulled me onto his lap and cradled me. "I'm terrified that I'm going to end up just like her, that's why I focused so hard on school, work, and finding good jobs. I guess that's why I'm still a virgin. If she wasn't addicted to alcohol it was men. She didn't stay clean until she met Derek and once he left she was right back on the booze. Why couldn't she do it for me? I never left her; I still take care of her!" I cried louder and Jack stroked my hair.

"My mother was, well, is a fan of the bottle as well," Jack said still stroking my hair. "She made some awful decisions. Decisions I know she regrets, but she's too proud to admit it. I used to hate her, but now I can see how sad she really is," Jack revealed. "I don't think you'll turn out like your mother if you don't want to. We shouldn't avoid turning into them, we should just try to be our own people." We sat in silence and when Jack heard steady breathing coming from me he lifted me off the floor and carried my sleeping body onto the bed. He pulled off my shoes and jacket, admiring my dress, before slipping me under the covers.

"You look gorgeous tonight, Vivie," he said before placing a soft kiss to my forehead.

CHAPTER NINETEEN

I woke up the next morning and pulled the covers tighter around me. Slowly last night came into focus and I sat upright in bed half expecting to see Jack. There was a knock on the door.

'Room service," said the voice behind the large white door. I walked over and opened it just a crack.

"I didn't order any room service," I said looking apologetically at the man with the trolley. He smiled and started wheeling in the cart.

"Your husband ordered it for you." I almost laughed at his mistake. "He also left this." The bellhop handed me an envelope and exited the room. I was starving and lifted the lid to reveal a full plate of eggs, bacon, pancakes, and fruit. He had also ordered me an array of juices and a large carafe of coffee. Drinking a cup before doing anything else, I finally settled on the bed popping pieces into my mouth as I opened the letter.

Dear Vivie,

I don't think last night turned out as either of us thought it would. I would like to request your presence at dinner this Monday at the Fair Ridge Restaurant, seven pm, to discuss our arrangement. If this doesn't work with your schedule please call me.

Jack

I read the letter over and over again, it was formal and curt with his number written neatly under his name. I thought back to the night we had spent together and from what I could remember he was sweet and patient with me. *OH GOD*, I thought, *I talked about mom!* I rubbed my hands across my face, I had never really opened up to anyone about my mom, only a few people from that time in my life were still in contact with me, and I would only admit the stories to people who had been there to witness the descent of Mary Allen. At least he wasn't disgusted with me. I hadn't exactly acted professionally. I couldn't understand how the Jack I had met the night before was the same man who had saved me and the same man who worked with Matt. Matt always talked about his business partner as if he were an old man. I wondered how many other versions of Jack I would get to meet before our deal was done.

$$$

"We didn't do it," I said into the phone. I parked my car in the crowded parking garage and moved to exit.

"What do you mean, you didn't do it?" asked Matt through the receiver. "Oh Ginny, you didn't freak out did you? It's alright if you did! I knew this would end badly, but hey at least we gave it a shot."

"No, no, I didn't freak out, It's just, it's complicated." I ran my hand through my hair. I walked down the sidewalk toward a giant sign that read "Benny's Diner". "I think it ended...fine," I lied. "We just didn't get around to doing it."

"Were you too busy discussing the weather? What happened?" Matt asked. I didn't want to tell him that it was because I got drunk. As I neared the diner I started looking around for Nick. "Don't worry I'll fix it," I said.

"Fix what?" Nick asked coming up behind me and wrapping me in a bear hug.

"I'll talk to you later." I said into the phone before hitting the end button.

"Hello, you!" I turned to face him still wrapped in his arms, "Just boring work stuff. How are you?"

"Starving," he said taking my hand and leading me through the diner door. I giggled as we moved to sit in a booth.

"I'm guessing work went ok?" I said.

"Yeah, everything has just been falling into place this week," he said. "What about you?

"Stressful, but nothing I can't handle," I said picking up the menu. We ordered our food and Nick, thankfully, kept the conversation light. I learned that Nick liked a wide range of movies and music, and I told him about the array of jobs I'd had growing up.

"When I moved here I got the job at Lion and Lamb," I finished.

"So what's your new job?" he asked. I paled not sure how to answer his question.

"Well I'm..." I started but was saved by the ringing of his phone. Nick looked at the screen to see who was calling him.

"I'm sorry I have to get this." Nick said standing and walking out of the door. He settled beside the diner door and exhaled a long breath before pushing a button and holding the phone to his ear.

Just tell him you're a boring assistant and if he asks deeper questions just say it's all filing and database maintenance, I thought. The waitress brought the food just as Nick came back in, catching her before she left.

"Hey, can we get some to go boxes?" he asked. I was confused as he sat back down in the booth. "Don't hate me, but I need to go."

Well that's vague, I thought.

"Oh, ok." I couldn't hide the irritation and disappointment in my voice. Rubbing his hands through his hair he looked up at me.

"My brother called me, the one that I'm not that close to. He asked me to grab a drink with him. I did something awhile ago that wasn't, I don't know, but he helped me out and he didn't have to." Nick said. I could see that he was struggling with how much to tell me.

"No worries, go have fun with your brother, I'll

be fine." I told him. I didn't know what to think. I was disappointed he was ditching me, but he needed to reconnect with his family. If I had that kind of opportunity I would jump at it too. We boxed up our burgers and he gave me a quick kiss on the cheek when we parted on the sidewalk.

I drove home alone and sat in the middle of my empty apartment as I ate my cold food. Pulling out my phone I texted the one person I had been avoiding talking to. Clicking on Jack's name I typed.

> **Hello Jack, I am available Monday at seven.**
> **– Vivie**

Short, sweet, and to the point. I was going to forget about all of the embarrassing details of the night before and be professional, just like Jack had been in his letter the morning after. I couldn't fuck this up, and I knew that normally I wouldn't have even gotten a second chance, mostly because I was sure all of Matt's usual clients would have no problems sleeping with a drunk prostitute. My phone beeped and I looked at the screen which proudly proclaimed Jack's name.

> **Good. See you then, Vivie.**
> **– Jack**

CHAPTER TWENTY

"Earth to Ginny," Matt said Monday morning, pulling slightly on my chair.

I was staring blankly at the computer screen and thinking about Jack. *No, it is not a date*, I thought. *You are dating Nick, not Jack! Jack just wants the sex. Nick wants the whole package and you want Nick's whole package and just Jack's money, not his package.*

"Hello in there!" Matt said again.

"Sorry, just thinking about, you know," I said laying my head on my folded arms. My phone beeped. I didn't have to look to know it was Nick texting me again. He had been relentless since our date at the diner. The first fourteen texts had been apologies for leaving our date early. I didn't know what to do. I spent the majority of Sunday going back and forth on whether or not I should keep this going. On the one hand Nick was charming, smart, practical, and incredibly handsome. On the other hand I felt horribly guilty every time I talked to him. Ignoring him much longer would inevitably lead to a decision being made for me. I needed an outside opinion and although I didn't really want to involve Matt anymore into my personal life, he was the only one I could really trust. My small face brightened as I realized that Matt was my best friend, in every sense of the word. Slowly lifting my head I turned toward him. "I need your advice...Boy advice." Matt laughed.

"You do know how weird this is right?" he asked. He let his smile fall and his face turned serious. "This isn't about Jack is it?"

"No, it's this guy I met a couple weeks ago. I really like him and he's really nice, but I just don't know if I can see him while doing this." I motioned my hands toward myself.

"What do you mean? You can't see him while you do some light filing?" Matt teased. "If he's nice to you and you really like him don't let your part time job get in the way."

"But I mean I can't tell him about it. He would freak out and I really don't want to lose him, before I even really have him."

"No you definitely shouldn't tell him but I don't see why it should be that big of a deal, you two aren't exclusive and it's not like you'll be doing it forever. If tonight goes as planned this won't even be a problem tomorrow," Matt said.

He has a point, I thought.

"Oh and please end it tonight! I think I'm getting an ulcer from my nerves. Jack has never participated in this side of the business," Matt finished.

That surprised me. I had assumed that Jack bid on all of the new girls. *There is a lot left to learn about Jack. Pity I won't have the time to figure him out*, I thought.

Thirty minutes later there was a knock on the door. Matt rushed past me to answer it.

"Thank you!" he said to the person I couldn't see behind the door. "I'll be back in a little bit, Ginny," he said letting Alice step into the room.

"Hey, Chica!" she said to me throwing herself onto the sofa. "So I hear you botched your first client." I groaned. Matt should know it's not good to gossip in this business.

"I didn't botch it… It's just been prolonged," I said.

"Well Matty wants me to teach you the art of seduction…" she said rolling her eyes. "I'm not exactly the teaching type so how about we just talk about some of the guys I've gone out with." Great! A day full of talking about sex with strangers and a night full of having sex with strangers.

$$$

I smoothed out my dress, one Matt had bought for me and walked up to the hostess at the Fair Ridge Hotel Restaurant. I could see the now infamous bar from my previous night here. The hostess led me through a door in the back. The small room had a fireplace to the right and a small table set for two arranged in the middle of the room. Jack wasn't there yet since I was once again very early. *I hope he has a room*, I thought. He surely wouldn't just bend me over the table. I didn't think he was that kind of guy, but then again he had already surprised me with his gentle response to my predicament the last time we met.

"I was hoping to arrive before you," Jack said startling me from my thoughts. "I thought this room would be beneficial for what we needed to discuss." Jack didn't look like the same man I had spent the night with a few days ago, he looked much older. He was still the same man who had held my hair back while I puked my guts out, but his crisp black suit made his handsome face seem cold and his deep green eyes held no warmth this time.

"I'm always early," I said explaining.

"That's a good habit," Jack said sitting opposite me. "How have you been?" he asked unfolding his napkin and placing it on his lap. I didn't know how to answer that. I had been confused, embarrassed, and not to mention a complete nervous wreck since the last time we had seen each other.

"Fine, you?" I said. *This is a business deal*, I thought, *no emotions allowed!* The waiter walked in but I wasn't sure if Jack had even noticed him. Jack was staring at me, his bold green eyes scrutinizing my every move as I squirmed under his stare.

"May I offer you a glass of wine?" the waiter had finished his rehearsed speech about the dinner specials. I flushed remembering the last time I drank at the Fair Ridge. Jack cocked an eyebrow up and a small smile graced one side of his mouth. I bit my bottom lip nervously and pulled my eyes from Jack to the waiter, shaking my head no.

"I don't think we'll be having any wine tonight." Jack said to the waiter still staring at me. The waiter moved to leave but Jack halted him. "We will have the house pasta tonight and two," he looked back at me, "Cokes." He finished and the waiter nodded and left.

"I hope you don't mind that I ordered for us." Jack said. I had a feeling that this new Jack I was meeting liked to order people around and make decisions for them. I felt very weak around him and I hated it.

"I would have preferred something with a little spice, but I'm sure whatever you ordered will be fine," I said wanting to be a part of the conversation and not just some wide eyed girl blindly agreeing to everything he said.

"I'm sure it will be spicy enough for you," Jack said. I wasn't entirely sure that we were talking about dinner anymore. I pushed down my nerves. I wasn't Ginny tonight; I was Vivie, the virgin vixen. I remembered the way Robin explained her methods for seducing her clients, not that they needed much seducing. I leaned slightly toward Jack giving him the best view of my cleavage, exposed in my black V-neck dress.

"You sound so sure. Can you read my mind?" I said sweeping my eyes across Jack's face and chest. "No, I don't think you can. If you could we wouldn't be ordering dinner at all," I said pulling my hair away from my face.

"Don't do that, I don't want this," he motioned at me. I raised my eyebrows shocked. I straightened. "You see, I could say," his voice went deeper, "We need to keep our strength up for what I have in mind for later." His voice returned to its natural octave. "but I don't want the overly sexy, porn star, woman, and I don't want to have to play a character myself," Jack explained.

"Well then what do you want?" I asked exasperated. My temper easily covered my embarrassment.

"You," Jack said with a smirk. That shocked me, he didn't even know me. Our waiter walked in carrying a large tray. He set down the large bowl of pasta in the center of the table and a long loaf of bread. He placed plates in front of both of us. Jack waved the waiter away before he could serve us. I looked at the boy trying to apologize with my eyes, but he didn't seem fazed, and he definitely didn't dare to look at me before he left. Jack's body language made it clear who the alpha was at this table, and it was clear it wasn't me. Standing, Jack served me first and then himself. He started to eat but I was still focused on what he just said.

"Why me?" I asked. I picked up my fork and started to push my food around my plate. *Why? Why did you ask that stupid question*, I said to myself, *there is only one reason he wants you and it's not for your brain*. "No don't answer that." I said. Jack continued to chew his food, and I continued to push mine around my plate hoping that he would start a conversation. Nothing serious need be said, but I would like, maybe, some casual banter. Instead, we both sat in silence while we ate. I didn't eat much. My nerves were getting harder and harder to push down. Jack noticed my unease.

"You don't have to do this," Jack said. His face was a stone wall, but his eyes scanned my face and body and soon they turned sympathetic. Great not only was I a whore, I was a whore who got pitied. "I mean we really don't have to do this if you don't want to," he mumbled staring into my eyes before quickly returning them to his plate. If I wasn't so angry I would be speechless. The god sitting across from me looked like a child caught with his hand in the cookie jar. I would never understand how one man could be so intimidating while also appearing so ashamed. Before I could have a chance to talk to him like a human being he added, "Of course you won't get paid." I felt the flush in my cheeks.

"I want to do this, so let's just do it!" I yelled. I was tired of people telling me I didn't have too. I needed to do it. Why didn't anyone else get it? "Do you have a room?" I paused for Jack's answer, he looked more shocked than upset.

"Yes" he said. The pity was gone from his eyes. A fire replaced it as he tried to pull himself together.

"Good let's go." I threw my napkin on the table and waited for Jack to stand. His mischievous smile had returned to his face as he stood and offered me his arm. I took it, and he led me out of our private dining room and toward the elevators. Stepping into the elevator Jack pushed the button marked fourteen, the same floor we were on last time. I wondered if we were staying in the same room. A few more people stepped into the elevator pushing Jack and me together. I could smell him, and I leaned in closer to him instinctively. I looked up at

Jack, taking in his strong features, as his eyes met mine. I had been caught staring. He smiled at me and we both continued to stare while people got on and off the elevator.

I couldn't stop looking at him. I was embarrassed at being caught, but being this close to him brought back a stir of feelings I had only felt during my dreams, and now I was staring into those green eyes again. *Maybe this was just a dream*, I thought. The real me was probably sleeping back in my apartment. The real me was probably still friends with Hailey and still worked at Lion and Lamb Salon. Hell, my real parents were probably still together in the suburbs living happily and sending me care packages. I felt Jack's hands on my waist as the people in the elevator shifted to accompany the increase and decrease of people. I couldn't help but remember the feeling of those large hands running up and down my body, the remembered sensations from my dreams seeped into the front of my mind and I couldn't push them away. I closed my eyes as I returned to my dream. Although in reality Jack's hands stayed firmly on my hips, the Jack I was imagining was moving them down my buttocks and the tops of my thighs. A man with a large suitcase stepped onto the elevator and Jack pulled me closer, his hands tightening on my hips as we pressed together. I remembered his weight pressing on top of me and the sensation of his hips settling between my legs teasing me. I remembered my dream like it was a memory. My body remembered his body. My arms rested on Jack's chest as he shielded me from the people on the elevator. His scent flooded my senses. A majority of the people got off the elevator at the next stop and Jack started to step away from me, but I grabbed onto his lapel to stop him as the elevator dinged and the last stranger got off leaving us alone. Jack tried to step back again, but this time I didn't let him move an inch. I wasn't following any rules or anecdotes from Robin's stories, I let him fill my senses.

Stepping on my tiptoes I leaned up and tried to kiss him, but I was too short. I waited for him to kiss me squeezing my eyes shut as I repeated my new found mantra in my head. *This is just a dream,* I could do it if it was just a dream. I closed my eyes tighter and pulled myself up using his collar.

"What are you doing?" Jack asked. I could feel his breath on my face his voice just a whisper. Moving my hands from his chest to around his neck I tried to get closer to him my eyes still firmly closed.

"Kiss me." I whispered. Jack moved his hands from my hips and wrapped them around my waist.

"Open your eyes," he said. We were so close now I could feel his nose touching mine. I tried to steal a kiss, but he was too fast and moved his head back out of my reach.

"Open your eyes, Vivie," he said again.

"No." I said. If I opened my eyes I would lose my nerve, I'd return to the frightened girl. He wanted the real me, but I couldn't give it to him. The real me would never accept money for sex, she would have never left Hailey, or gotten black out drunk with strangers. I didn't know who I was turning into, but I knew if I didn't do this with Jack I would never be able to turn into the person I wanted to be, and to turn into that girl, I needed a degree.

Jack surprised me by lifting me up and wrapping my legs around his hips. He walked until my back was against the elevator wall and the cold metal momentarily shocked me, sending chills up my spine.

"Who are you thinking about?" Jack asked an aggressive tone taking over his deep rich voice. He pushed his hips into me and my breath quickened. I started to shake in anticipation and faintly heard the dinging of the elevator, the memory of his eyes were still burning in the front of my mind.

"You," I said breathless. Jack kissed me hard, my mouth moving against his in an unspoken rhythm. He lifted me, carrying me off the elevator and to our room. He effortlessly unlocked the door while still holding me. I mindlessly kissed him grating my hips against his as he moved us through the room. Jack paused in front of the bed, while I compared the dream Jack and the real Jack in my head. I unwrapped my legs and slid down his chest slowly unbuttoning the buttons beneath his black tie. I pulled off his shirt and let it drop to the floor. Jack took his time slowly running his hands up and down my body as he took off my dress. A pang of self-consciousness hit me along with the cold air as my dress touched the floor. Jack slowly lowered me onto the bed and breaking away from our kiss he started a trail of kisses down my cheek, my neck, and my collarbone. I grabbed for him and he returned to my lips. His body warmed mine as he rested himself on top of me. I ran my hands down the side of his chest and scratched my way up his back. Jack shifted and slightly lifted me off the bed. He unhooked my bra and slid it from my arms. When he lowered me to the bed he slid down my body and took one nipple in his mouth licking and biting it until it was hard, before moving to the other breast and repeating his path. I squirmed underneath him.

"Jack," I breathed as he pinched and rolled one sensitive nipple between his fingers. I raised my hips up grinding against him trying to find a release for the building pressure in my core. Jack kissed me again, tangling one hand in my hair while the other slowly made its way down my chest and stomach. Slipping his hand between my legs, he rubbed me over my panties. Surprised I opened my eyes. I pulled Jack closer, vaguely aware that I was shaking from head to toe. I didn't care if it was a dream anymore. I only knew that I didn't want it to stop.

"Jack," I said again with urgency in my voice, Jack lifted himself off the bed and began undoing his pants. *Damn*, I thought, looking over his body. He was standing at my feet in only his dark gray boxer briefs. *I hope I'm not awful at this*, I thought, *shut up brain*! I couldn't stop shaking, I wasn't sure if it was from my nerves, the cold, or the anticipation. Jack kicked off his pants and bent over me again. His mischievous smile faded into first confusion and then anger.

"I can't do this." he said straightening. He grabbed his clothes and walked into the bathroom shutting the door loudly.

I sat up confused and still riled up. I looked at the closed bathroom door and back down at my semi naked body. *Maybe this was a dream*, I thought, *It sure ended like one.*

CHAPTER TWENTY-ONE

Jack had been in the bathroom for over an hour. In that time I had heard him break something, yell, and take a very long shower. I wasn't really concerned with what he was doing. I was too focused on my own rage.

Since his abrupt departure I had gone from confused, to embarrassed, to angry. Why did he stop? Why was I so eager to sleep with a perfect stranger? I convinced myself that this was some sort of prostitution loophole. No penetration no payment. Thirty minutes after Jack's change of conscience I was sure he had gone to beat it off in the bathroom. I channeled my unreleased energy and started pacing the space in front of the bathroom door. *Things are not ending like this. I should at least get half!* I thought. My phone started to buzz and I reached down to answer it.

"Hello." I said. I didn't recognize the number.

"Vivie? It's Jack."

"Really? Really?" I yelled throwing my phone at the bathroom door. "Face me like a man, Jack!" I shouted at the room. He opened the door a sliver, holding a corded phone in his hand. "Calling from the bathroom? Really?" I yelled.

"I didn't think you were still here," he said hanging up the receiver. "I wouldn't have blamed you if you left."

"I'm in this, and if you're not, then tell me now because this isn't just a game to me. I need to do this." I said.

"I wanted to do it, you could tell how much I wanted to, but I couldn't," Jack said.

"It's a little late to grow a conscience," I mumbled sitting on the bed. Jack picked my dress up off the floor and handed it to me. I was still half naked and I threw the dress on over my head getting my arms tangled in the complicated straps. He helped me straighten and pull down the dress. "I can do it," I said standing to smooth the fabric. "I'm not a child."

"I know you're not a child," Jack said exasperated. "and I'm not a monster! You were, you were shaking and I couldn't," Jack paused to run his hands through his hair. "It shouldn't be like this for you. I can't just take this from you. I need you to trust me. Do you trust me?" Jack asked. All cool strength fell from his eyes and all that was left was his concern. He looked so vulnerable.

"Do I trust a total stranger who has offered to pay a ridiculous amount of money for my virginity?" I scoffed while Jack winced. "Money buys a lot of things, but trust isn't one of them," I said sitting back on the bed. Jack sat next to me and put his head in his hands.

"Ok, so you would feel more comfortable if you got to know me better?" Jack said. I looked at him incredulously.

"Jack, it's—" I started.

"Hear me out." Jack said sensing my hesitance. "What if we went out on some mock dates or something?" he asked hopefully. I laughed and laid back on the bed, Jack reclined next to me.

"A date? Like, what? Have a three date rule or something?" I laughed again turning to face him. He was completely serious, his eyes were pleading with me to hear him out.

"Exactly. We could schedule dates and on the last date we do it," he said. There were a number of reasons I should say no, but I couldn't. The business man Jack had disappeared and the gentle, kind man had returned. I was less than excited to realize I was actually looking forward to seeing him again.

"Ok," I said. What was I getting myself into? Matt was going to be furious.

"Ok," Jack said, more to himself than me. He turned to look at me and I basked in his easy smile longer than I should have.

"So does this count as our first date?" I asked, flicking my eyes to the ceiling.

"God, I hope not. If it does then this was a pretty shitty date," he said laughing. "For our first date I'll…" Jack paused and didn't finish his thought.

"What?" I asked leaning on my elbow to look at him better.

"Nothing, never mind."

"You can't do that!" I said, playfully smacking him on the chest. He grabbed my hand and held it gently where it landed.

"I want it to be a surprise." I smiled at him before turning to look at the clock.

"It's almost one, I better get home," I said, snaking my hand out from under his. I got up and grabbed my things. "Email me your schedule and we can plan our dates." I said. Jack got up and grabbed his jacket. We both headed out of our room and into the elevator. Jack pushed the button for the garage.

"Let me drive you home," he said. "I promise I won't try anything." I laughed and nodded. Jack opened the car door for me and I sat back in his very nice sports car. He navigated the streets with ease. I told him my address and he parked in the drive.

"Will you be alright getting in?" Jack asked.

"Yea" I said. I should have been excited to be home, but my apartment was so empty and it still didn't feel like home to me even though I had unpacked and scattered numerous personal knick-knacks throughout the place. "Do you wanna come in?" I asked.

"Are you trying to get into my pants, Vivie?" Jack said with a laugh. I smiled back. I knew I was sending mixed signals.

"I just moved in here and it's," I paused, "I don't know. I'm sorry." I turned and shook my head a little pulling at the handle to release the door.

"What's wrong?" Jack put his hand on my arm to stop me.

"It's nothing." I cemented the smile on my face, but it didn't reflect my true feelings. "Thank you for the ride." I got out of the car and walked in. I noticed Jack didn't pull away until I was safely behind the locked door. I rode the elevator to my floor and my phone pinged as I pulled out my keys.

How'd it go? –Matt

Fine. –Ginny

Good. You OK? –Matt

Yep. See you tomorrow. –Ginny

Okay. Jack transferred the money. I'll have your cut by Weds. – Matt

I didn't know what to think about that. Jack must have paid before we made our little arrangement. I also didn't know why I wasn't telling Matt the whole truth. I would eventually have to tell him about the three date plan, but I almost liked having a secret between Jack and me. I changed out of my dress and climbed into my large bed. I hugged a pillow to my chest and closed my eyes, excited about what was waiting for me in my dreams.

CHAPTER TWENTY-TWO

Hello Vivie,

I am available every Thursday night for the next three weeks. Let me know if those days don't work for you.

Jack

I read his email over and over again. He sounded like the stern business man he must have portrayed at his job, and not the confused, gentle, patient, man-boy he turned into around me.

"No phones!" Robin said from the other side of the couch. I turned it on vibrate and hid it under my thigh.

"She's a very busy professional, Robin!" Michael said squeezing himself between us. I smacked him playfully.

"I'm glad you cancelled the party tonight," I said

snuggling into his side. "A quiet sleepover is what I needed. No drama!" Michael squirmed uncomfortably and glanced at Robin. "What?" I asked confused.

"Nick called me a couple days ago." Michael said. I had been avoiding Nick, partly because I was guilty over my weird relationship with Jack and partly because I was still upset with him for ditching me at the diner. He called and texted a few times since then and when I didn't ignore his calls I was short with him. The similarities between Jack and Nick were unnerving at times. They both ran hot and cold giving and withholding information from me. I couldn't blame them, Jack was blurring the lines between business arrangement and relationship while I was blurring the lines with Nick. I liked Nick. He was the smart choice, but not one I thought I could handle. "He's coming over tonight for the sleepover," Michael said. I smiled sadly. I knew I couldn't commit to Nick the way he needed me to and while I hoped our relationship would slowly fall away Nick was hell bent to make it work.

The doorbell rang and Michael squeezed my knee before rising to answer it. Nick walked in looking perfect like he always did. I quickly closed my eyes, I needed to stop staring at him before I finished mentally undressing him. I took a deep breath before feeling something brush my leg. When I peeped one eye open I froze. Nick's face was only inches from mine as he squatted down to my eye level.

"Are you alright?" he whispered. My breath

caught in my chest and I could only see him, only smell him. Robin and Michael must have been holding their breaths, too, because it was only Nick I could hear.

"Yea, I'm fine," I said unable to move.

"Can we talk?"

"Yea, sure." Nick moved back from me and I started to stand turning away from Michael and Robin. We walked into the hall and paused a few doors away from Michael's apartment.

I had some vague ideas about what Nick wanted to discuss, but I braced myself for the inevitable. I knew I couldn't keep leading him on like this. I knew it had to end at some point.

"So you've been avoiding me," Nick said as I stared down at my hands. "Any particular reason why?" he asked. I still couldn't tell him about Jack or about the arrangement I had made with Matt. I tore my eyes from my hands and looked into Nick's sad worried eyes.

"I can't be in a serious relationship right now Nick. There are too many things exploding around me, and I don't think it would be fair to drag you into the fire," I said. Nick looked relieved which stung a little. Part of me wanted him and his seemingly un-dramatic life.

"That's all?" Nick said laughing. Anger flashed through my body and I rolled my eyes at him turning back toward the apartment. Before I had finished taking a step he stopped me. "I'm sorry, it's… never mind. It's a lot better than what I thought you were going to say." He rubbed my arm and the anger started to recede. "I'm not accepting that though. Everyone deals with the shit life throws at them. I want to be a part of your shit storm." That was romantic... kind of... it didn't change the fact that until I sealed the deal with Jack there wasn't going to be much of a relationship between Nick and me.

"That's sweet, Nick, really, but I just don't think it'll work."

"Why? Did I completely read the signs wrong? Do you not like me?" he said cocking one of his eyebrows.

"You know I like you," I said

"Then be with me."

"I can't." This was starting to get old.

"Why?" he asked.

Why? I thought. *Well Nick I can't date you because I have to sleep with this guy, Jack... for money, and that's all I'm capable of thinking about right now.*

"Because," I said aloud defeated.

"I'm gonna lay it all out right now, Ginny, because I can't keep going back and forth with you. I can't keep doing what we've been doing, and I know that if you don't just give in and be my girl then we are just going to continue the twisted date-hookup-avoid triangle we've been doing since the beginning." He was exasperated and had stopped moving his hand up and down my arm. I knew he was right and I knew that I wouldn't be able to stop myself when he was in the room. I craved his energy and his honesty.

"I don't love you," he continued, "but I know I could. Everything in my body is telling me to fight for you, to fight to get you, and I know I'm not the most open person, but neither are you. I can see the secrets behind every lie and change of subject you make, but from here on out I'm an open book for you. Ask me anything and I will tell you the truth no matter how hard it will be," he paused catching his breath. I could feel his hand was moist where it touched my arm. I knew I should keep my mouth shut but a part of me wanted to test him.

"How many BIG secrets do you have?" I asked. Nick thought for a moment the serious expression never leaving his face.

"One, well, two technically," he said not elaborating. I smiled, Nick and I were so similar and I knew I would have to ask all the right questions if I ever wanted the whole story. Nick braced himself for the inevitable next question. *What are they?* But I couldn't ask him that. I couldn't take a piece of him without giving a piece of myself.

"I'm willing to roll with your punches, Ginny, give me a shot." His eyes showed emotions he was keeping from his face and I briefly wondered if he didn't already love me. The thought scared and excited me, I had never been loved before, not even by the people who were supposed to love you no matter what. Why couldn't I have it all? I was only interested in Jack because of his money right? Jack was only nice to me because he wanted my body, right? Nick wanted my mind and all of the horrible things I kept locked up inside of it. Maybe I could have the money and the picket fence.

"Ok," I said before I could yet again talk myself

out of it.

"Ok?" Nick asked a little taken aback.

"Yes, but we need to take it slow, you may be an open book but," I stalled not knowing how to say that I couldn't share all of me with him yet, not all of my body or of my mind.

"I understand," he said before I could finish. "I'll wait for your secrets, but I need you to understand that I'll need to know them one day. I mean eventually I want there to be no secrets between the two of us." I lowered my head and nodded. "But I'm fine with that being in the far, far, distant future." He laughed and as I cracked a smile I couldn't help but wonder what his secrets were, and if they were even close to the bombshells I had.

We walked back into Matt's apartment holding hands. We sat together and talked all through the movie, well, until Robin and Michael threw handfuls of popcorn at us.

"Shut Up!" they yelled in unison. Nick and I fell asleep side by side.

CHAPTER TWENTY-THREE

I wasn't nearly as nervous about my date with Jack as I was before. I was with Nick and happier now that he was in my life. Nick had a way of making me forget that the sky was falling. I just had to keep reminding myself that Jack was not interested in me in the long term. Matt was out of the apartment when I arrived for work. When I had finished all of my daily tasks I noticed a stack of papers that had needed to be either mailed or delivered. I walked down the street heading toward Eagle Fort Towers. I was on my last stop, delivering a large manila envelope to a Mr. Eagle. I walked through the familiar doors, laughing, as I noticed a particularly attractive man talking to Michael. One of his many admirers, I assumed. He saw me and excused himself to walk over and give me a hug.

Releasing me he asked, "What are you doing here? Come to visit?"

"Dropping off a package for Matt," I said

indicating the envelope.

"Oh," he said eyeing the package. "What is it? I bet it's drugs, is it drugs?" he asked. I whacked him in the arm with the envelope.

"It's not drugs, I don't know what it is," I laughed. "It's for a Mr. Eagle, let me check what suite."

"Oh God, I hope it's drugs. That guy is so stiff! He needs to get laid or something," he whispered guiding me behind the turnstiles. "If it's not drugs do us all of favor and let him slip it in, I mean I would, but..." he didn't get a chance to finish before I started hitting him hard with the envelope. "I was joking!" he said leading me to the elevators.

"So, what's his deal?" I asked knowing it was none of my business.

"He's a big shot at Miller Cove, need I say more?" he said. I couldn't stop myself from scowling.

"Oh great I wonder if I'll get harassed in person today as opposed to over the phone," I groaned.

"Just look on the bright side," Michael started, "You don't have to start paying them for a while and then when you do have to pay them and you can't afford it, it's not like they can take anything away from you... because you don't own anything." I swung at him again but he dodged to push the call button for the elevator. "Stop that," he said batting the envelope away. The elevator doors dinged open. "Okay, you are going to take this to the top floor. When you hit reception ask for Melissa, and she'll take the package," he said moving out of the way.

"Thanks, Michael, if I'm not back in thirty

minutes, send the police," I said laughing as the doors closed. The ride up was longer than I thought it would be. The doors opened up into a spacious reception area. As I stepped upto the desk, while the woman behind it held up a finger for me to wait. She ended the call and expectantly waited for me to address her.

"Hi, I'm looking for Melissa I have a package for Mr. Eagle," I said.

"Go down the hall," she said pointing to her left. "it's the last door on the right." The phone rang again and she immediately answered it. Her voice changed from the annoyed version I had been greeted with to a cheery almost ear splitting tone. I thanked her and headed down the hall noticing people working in their offices, through the large glass windows that lined the walls. Reaching the last office, I knocked on the closed door.

"Come in," a sweet voice said from inside the room. I turned the knob stepping into the office. The door pushed against me as it tried to automatically close. I stopped to take in the large room. There was a couch immediately to my left with a mini fridge, coffee table, and chair surrounding it. Opposite it was a large wooden desk with two high backed chairs for visitors, behind the desk stood a woman.

"Hello," she said cheerily, "How can I help you?" I hastily crossed the space to stand in front of her desk. Taking in her bright dress and sunny disposition, I was a little annoyed that she could be so happy working for a company that caused me so much stress.

"Hi, I'm dropping off a package for Mr. Eagle." I said trying to sound professional.

"Ok, I can go ahead and take it." I lifted up the envelope and started to hand it to her. Her fingers closed on the package as the door behind her opened. I froze locking my fingers around the envelope. Melissa tugged a little on the golden packet before turning to look at what I was staring at. The two men standing in the door animatedly shaking hands didn't faze her at all, she saw this sort of behavior daily, but she wasn't currently in a cash for sex relationship with one of them. Jack was standing in the doorway in a black suit and a grey tie that made his eyes glow. With a final tug Melissa freed the envelope from my grasp. I was still staring at Jack, and from the corner of my eye I could see Melissa shaking her head. She was probably used to women ogling her boss on the daily.

"Thank you, do I need to sign anything?" she asked trying to pull my attention away from her incredibly attractive boss. Jack noticed my staring then. He had to do a double take before he finally realized who I was. I think I went white all over and then immediately turned red. "Are you alright?" Melissa asked.

"Not really," I said breaking my eyes away from Jack who had moved from the door to escort the man from the room. I could hear them talking behind me. Silently I started to back up.

"Sorry, thank you," I whispered to Melissa. *Why am I whispering?* I thought. Turning away from her, I let my hair fall down around my face trying to create a barrier between me and the world. I avoided looking in Jack's direction as I tried to sneak past him. He had closed the door after his guest had left and turned toward me. He caught me by the elbow as I swerved to avoid him. The familiar rush flowed through me at his touch.

"Come," he whispered harshly, as he walked toward the door from which he had appeared.

"Your mail, Mr. Eagle." Melissa said handing him the stack containing my envelope. He took it with his free hand. Melissa didn't even bat an eye over the scene that had just silently unfolded in front of her. Jack rushed me into the room and slammed the door closed.

"What the hell are you doing here?" he yelled, turning to face me.

"Delivering mail," I said instantly going on the defensive. "What the hell are you doing here?" I asked back.

"I work here, which is exactly why you shouldn't be here."

"Which is exactly why I was trying to leave when you pulled me in here," I yelled at him. Both of our voices were raised and we were getting closer to each other the louder we yelled.

"Fine, then go!" he yelled.

"Fine, I will!" I yelled, heading back to the door. "By the way, you work for a bunch of assholes!" I said, my hand on the door. I heard a small laugh escape Jack's lips. "What?" I asked, turning to face him, hands on my hips.

"I work for my mother," he said. I turned beet red. Not knowing what else to say I just shrugged.

Mother or not, I still thought everyone working for the company was an ass, except Jack of course. I knew he was an ass. Turning back towards the door I twisted the knob. But before I could open it, Jack's hands were pushing the door to keep it closed. I turned to face him, knowing he was far too close to me. My body was betraying my mind as anticipation fluttered my stomach and my breathing increased.

"What are you doing Jack?" I asked shakily.

"Seeing if you trust me," he said.

"Nope," I answered, turning to face him and harshly laughing in his face.

"And what is your reason for not trusting me today?" he smiled.

"I don't know, maybe because you work for the devil?" I said.

"Watch it," he said, his sexy smirk still slathered on his face. "What did Miller Cove ever do to you?" He was leaning so close to me that his intoxicating smell filled the space around me. A light bulb went off in my head and before he could react I kissed him hard. He kissed me back just as eagerly and I steered us toward his desk. Backing him into it he released his hands from my hair and absentmindedly tossed papers on the floor. Once the remnants of his desk were scattered around our feet I pushed him down on the, now empty, desk. He leaned back and closed his eyes as I trailed kisses down his chest. When I unbuckled his belt he kicked off his shoes. I unbuttoned his pants and he lifted his hips so I could ease them off. His eyes were still closed.

"I guess you're warming up to us here at Miller Cove," he said. He opened his eyes when he realized I had stopped my journey down his chest. I was already by the door, which was now cracked open. He started to sit as I stuffed his newly folded pants into my jacket. I tossed his wallet and keys onto the table.

"Miller Cove gave me false expectations," I said, as I opened the door and walked out.

CHAPTER TWENTY-FOUR

Oh God what did I just do? I just pantsed the man who is paying for my education. I riled him up and then stole his pants while he was at work! I flew out of the building, not even stopping to say goodbye to Michael. My phone blinked in my pocket. Whipping it out I saw Michael's name.

What happened? You ok?
– Michael

Yea fine, just in a hurry
– Ginny

I stowed my phone and it immediately buzzed again. *Didn't Michael ever work at his job*, I thought. But when I looked down, it wasn't Michael's name on my screen. It was Jack's.

Very funny Vivie. See you
tonight – Jack

My stomach sank to the floor as I realized it was Thursday.

$$$

Oh, hell yea, I was nervous. I dressed for the evening and found an old bag to put Jack's pants in. I kept alternating the bag between my hands on the ride up the elevator. When it dinged on the fourteenth floor I stepped around the other passengers and made my way off, and to the door. Realizing I didn't get a room key, I tentatively knocked. An old couple walked by me as the door opened. Jack was fully dressed and held out his hand for his pants. I handed the bag over and he stepped aside to let me in. I waited for him to say something but he was silent. He set the bag on the desk and turned to me. I squirmed under his intense stare. Why did he make me feel like a naughty child?

Not able to stand the awkward silence any longer I said, "So, how was your day?" His smirk returned.

"Interesting," he replied, "Yours?"

I shrugged, "Nothing special."

That got his attention. He moved from the desk to sit next to me on the bed. I couldn't stop myself from laughing. "I'm sorry," I choked out. Focused on my own laughter I didn't notice what Jack was doing. In one quick movement he had me pinned underneath him on the bed. He didn't kiss me, didn't even touch me, until I felt the weight of his body firmly push down on me. It didn't hurt, he was warm and firm and my body melded to his like it was meant to be there. My breath quickened as I took in his scent. Noses almost touching, he ran his hand down my cheek.

"I don't know why you don't trust me. Your body trusts me. Can you feel what I do to you?" he asked, his breath husky.

I squirmed under him and looked into his eyes. They didn't hold the same emotions as his words. They were sad and I realized that he was upset with me for playing the joke on him, however unplanned. I knew what he meant about being around someone who was playing a character. I felt myself reaching my hand up to cup his cheek.

"Who's playing the seductor now?" I asked.

He rolled off of me and sighed.

"I'm sorry I laughed at you... and stole your pants," I said as I turned to face him.

"It's alright, I'm just not used to being the butt of the joke," he said.

"I can tell," I mumbled. "I didn't know it was your office. If I had, I wouldn't have come."

"Yea, I'd be lying if I said it was normal for an escort to meet me at work," he said, subtly reminding me that we weren't friends. Ouch. I had let myself forget for a moment that he was not my friend, that I was in fact getting paid to be here. Hearing him say it was like having the rug pulled out from under me, setting it on fire, and then replacing it under me again. I didn't care that he was a john, and I didn't think of him as one either.

"I don't think any of this is normal," I said.

Jack grabbed my hand as we both laid back on the bed. He rubbed his thumb across the smooth skin. We laid there for what seemed like forever, both caught up in our own thoughts. Jack laughed a little. It was a sad sound and I turned to look at him. Noticing he had gotten my attention he said, "We are awful at dating."

I couldn't help the laugh that escaped. "I wouldn't know," I said. "I haven't been on many dates."

This perked his attention and I rolled my eyes before leaning up on my elbow. "Growing up I didn't really have time for dating. I was kind of a bookworm.... Still am actually." I laughed at myself. I saw the light shining through his eyes. I didn't want him to stop looking at me like that so I continued.

"Recent dates have mainly focused on eating," I said as he laughed. "Oh and watching movies, but I don't mind that as much. I love getting lost in a good story." I thought about every date Nick and I had organized and it always started with food. I started laughing.

"Oh yea? Been on a lot of dates recently?" he asked.

"Yea" I said, still laughing.

"Do you have a boyfriend?" he asked.

"Yea," I stopped laughing. Oh God, why would I admit that? What the hell was I thinking? I was getting too comfortable with him again.

"What's his name?" Jack asked. But I was still

reeling from the fact I had mentioned Nick at all. I just shook my head.

"What's he do for a living?" he tried again.

"Why? Jealous?" I said. Jack turned to look back up at the ceiling.

"Maybe."

I turned to look back at the ceiling too. What was I doing?

"So, Vivie," he turned toward me, the dangerous sparkle back in his eyes. "You know my name, where I work, and a plethora of details about my family. Do I get to learn anything about you?" he asked.

"Genevieve," I said as I turned back towards him. "That's my name." I looked back to the ceiling. We were still holding hands and Jack resumed running his thumb up and down the back of mine.

"Genevieve?" he said. I know I shouldn't have told him, but I felt like I owed him something. My real name was the least I could give him.

"Yes, Jack Eagle?"

"Would you like to watch a movie with me," he paused, "and not eat food?" he laughed.

I smiled. "I would love to."

Jack let me pick the movie. I chose a weird looking indie film from the list. By the end of it I was a sobbing mess and Jack was gently snoring. My phone started buzzing inside my bag. The screen told me it was almost 3a.m. as well as flashing Nick's name. Stepping into the bathroom I answered.

"Hey Nick. I can't really...." I started before

being cut off.

"Ginny? Hey it's Max from the bar. Sorry I didn't know who to call, but Nick's heading to the hospital. There was a fight and he got pretty fucked up." My heart pounded in my chest. I had so many questions for Max, but I could only force one from my throat.

"Which hospital?" I could hear the sirens in the background. The whining of them only making my heart beat faster.

"St. Alphonsus," he said, his voice straining not to crack.

"I'm on my way."

CHAPTER TWENTY-FIVE

I obsessively checked my phone as I walked into the hospital. I had left the hotel without stopping to leave a note for Jack. Max was pacing the Emergency Room waiting area.

"What happened?" I asked, running over to him. We hugged, which said something, because Max and I weren't exactly on hugging terms. Max was shaking his head as he looked at me.

"I don't know, some of the crowd was getting rowdy and he went over to calm them down. The next thing I know chairs and tables went flying," he said.

"Is he ok? Have the doctors talked to you?" I noticed some bruising on Max's face and looked down at his bloodied knuckles.

"No, I don't know. I jumped into the fight and pulled him out. He wasn't conscious. By the time everyone calmed down, the cops were there and Nick was in the ambulance." He let out a slow breath. "Ben rode with him. He's back there now."

"Are you ok?" I asked, stepping closer to look at his bruised face.

"Yea, I'm fine," he said, stepping back. We both moved to sit in the chairs lined up across the wall. I couldn't help the guilt that washed over me at not being there tonight. I usually spent most of my nights hanging at the bar with Nick and the boys. I know I couldn't have done anything, but the fact that I was with Jack while Nick had been hurt weighed heavily on me.

Michael and Robin walked through the doors a minute later. We filled them in, and we all just sat waiting for news.

"Dude, how is he?" Max shot out of the chair as Ben walked out from behind the double doors.

"He's fine," Ben lied. "A concussion and a couple of bruised ribs. And he dislocated his shoulder. It looks worse than it is," he laughed. "His face is totally fucked though. Adam got him in the face with a chair." We all cringed. "We can go back one at a time. They're keeping him overnight," he finished.

We all looked at each other, and then all eyes settled on me.

"Come on, Ginny," Ben said, putting his hand on the small of my back while guiding me through the doors. He left me at the entrance to Nick's room and I knocked before turning the handle. Nick was talking on the phone but quickly ended it as he saw me. One of his many secrets, I thought to myself.

"Hey," he said, sitting up a little. His face was swollen and purple with a bandage over his right eye. His shoulder and arm hung in a sling.

"Come here," he said. I hadn't realized I was frozen in the doorway. Tears spilled down my face as I walked toward him and threw my arms around him. Nick rubbed my back soothingly.

"Hey, it's ok. I'm fine. Nothing a night in the hospital won't fix," he assured me.

I knew these weren't just tears of sadness about what happened to Nick. These were tears of guilt. He held me while I cried and I pulled away, hating that he was comforting me, hating that I was crying because I was guilty.

"Do you need anything?" I asked, wiping my eyes with the hospital tissues.

"No I'm pretty much set. Ben is running back to the house to grab my stuff," he said.

"Do you want me to call anyone?" I asked.

"Already did," he said, rubbing my arm.

"Can I come in?" Max said, peeking his head around the door.

"Sorry, I'm hogging you," I said. "If you need me I'll be in the waiting room"

Nick shook his head. "No, you don't have to stay, really, go home and sleep. I'll call you in the morning."

I hesitated. "Ok." I wouldn't be much help to him in the waiting room. He flinched as I kissed him goodbye.

The floodgates reopened the second the door closed. I steadied myself on the wall. I don't even think I was crying about Nick anymore. Well, not solely about Nick. I was crying for everyone; my parents, Hailey, Nick, Jack. I checked my phone again and quickly shoved it back in my pocket. Nick was in the hospital and I was still thinking about Jack! I could even hear his voice. Turning my head violently side to side, I tried to shake out the sound of him, the thought of him, but before I could, he appeared. A few feet away, Jack stood talking to a nurse at the front desk. *Oh my God, did he follow me?* I looked for a possible escape route but had to settle with hiding behind a food trolley. The nurse, accompanied by Jack, moved down the hallway past the cart. *Where was he going?* I didn't get a chance to see where before a stern cough pulled my attention up. A middle aged woman was looking down at me.

"Hi." I said still squatting. Looking around I noticed Jack and the nurse were gone. "Just making sure the food here is good enough for my man." *Oh God, stop brain, stop mouth, just stop.* "Everything looks good!" I said to the still silent woman, who looked at me like I had escaped from the psych ward. I quickly stood and left, not giving her the chance to ask questions or call for security. Once I reached the waiting room I was a wreck, looking over my shoulder and around every corner for Jack. Michael and Robin were missing so I walked out to my car.

Where are you? – Ginny

I sent the message to Robin hoping that I wouldn't have to go searching for them.

Looking at babies come join! - Robin

I had no idea where the maternity ward was and had absolutely no desire to run into Jack.

**No thanks. Heading home text
me tomorrow. - Ginny**

I drove home and pulled into my parking spot exhausted. I rested my head on the wheel. Why was Jack at the hospital? He was sound asleep when I left so I am pretty sure he didn't follow me, unless he is a very good sleep actor. I let myself worry about Jack and Nick for a few more minutes, before I tried and failed to push him out of my head.

$$$

The ringing woke me and I jolted up. I was still in my car, having fallen asleep while thinking of ways to deal with Nick and Jack. My neck and back burned when I moved them and the clock on my dash told me I had slept the whole night cramped in the small space. It was nine a.m. and the insistent ringing drove my attention to the phone. I looked at the display and smiled.

"Hey, Maggie, long time no talk." I said groggily. Maggie had moved from Illinois to Arizona after high school, but we tried to get together whenever we could.

"Hey, Ginny, are you going to be home Wednesday?" she asked. I could hear people in the background.

"No, I wasn't planning on it why?" I asked

confused.

"Well… because Thursday is Thanksgiving… I thought you always went home for the holidays."

"Oh my God, I didn't even realize." I said smacking my hand on my head. "Well yea I guess I'll have to."

"Great, the gang's going out on Wednesday, I will text you details," she said excited.

"OK, thanks, Mags. I've gotta go to work but I'll let you know when I get into town," I said.

"OK, excited to see you!"

"Me too!" I answered. "Bye."

"Bye."

Shit! How could I forget about Thanksgiving? Although I hated the idea of cancelling on Jack when now more than ever I just wanted to get it over with, I needed to check on mom and I wanted to see my old friends again, while still being able to avoid Hailey.

I pulled out a scrap of paper and a pen. I had some major issues to take care of.

1. I needed to reschedule with Jack.

2. Call and check on Nick.

3. Tell Matt I haven't slept with Jack yet… and also about our three date rule… and I should probably mention that I stole his pants, or maybe not.

CHAPTER TWENTY-SIX

To say that Matt was upset would be an understatement. After berating me verbally, he hovered fuming for a solid thirty minutes, finally huffing off saying I needed to dig myself out of this hole! *Thanks Matt I'm fully aware of my fuck-ups,* I said in my head. One thing done on my checklist. I opened my email account and clicked compose, ignoring my full inbox, and started to type

Jack,

I have a conflict this Thursday. I forgot that it was Thanksgiving and I will be out of town. I am available Monday, Tuesday, and Friday through Sunday if you would like to reschedule.
Sorry for the inconvenience,
Vivie

Yea, I know it sounded a little too professional, but that's what our relationship was...right? I kept forgetting that Jack and I aren't boyfriend and girlfriend. Hell, we aren't even friends. My false feelings for him were only clouding my real feelings for Nick. Nick was my boyfriend and I cared for him deeply. I clicked send and stared at the pile of work Matt had laid out for me. Before diving into it I pulled out my phone. I scrolled through my contacts and clicked on Nick's name. After a few rings he answered.

"Hey, how ya feeling?" I asked trying to sound chipper after the mess I was the night before.

"I'm doing alright, just got home. How are you?" he asked.

I laughed before answering. "I'm not still crying, if that's what you're asking."

"Good," he laughed, "What are you doing this weekend? I'm leaving for Georgia on Tuesday and I was thinking you might like to spend it with me."

Smiling I said, "I couldn't think of a better way to spend my days."

"Good," he said. I couldn't stop smiling into the phone. I heard Matt in the background and lowered my voice.

"I have to go, sorry, I'm at work. Call me tomorrow?" I asked.

"Will do, have fun." he said chuckling into the phone.

"Get some sleep." I said noting his raw voice.

"Okay," he yawned.

"Okay. Good." I knew I should put the phone

down but I couldn't. Was he really alright? Was I awful for not being there?

"Bye," he said still laughing at me.

"Bye," I put the phone down and Matt threw himself on the couch behind me.

"I feel like shit," he said.

"Why?" I asked trying to organize the pile into a manageable state.

"You!" he said. "You're giving me an ulcer!" he yelled, lifting his head off the pillow. *What a drama queen.* I walked to the couch and forced him to scoot over so I could lay down next to him. Teetering on the edge I wrapped my arms around his middle.

"I will fix it. Actually I don't think it's really that broken." Matt looked at me skeptically. "I was nervous and he could sense that. The whole dates idea was him. I was just trying to please the client." I couldn't stop myself from smiling. Matt groaned before letting a small laugh escape.

"Hate me?" I asked. Matt looked me over.

"No." he said wrapping his arm around my shoulders.

"Good, now I have to get back to work before my boss fires me." I shifted to get up, but Matt wouldn't release me.

"No, I don't want to work today can we just hang? Watch a movie or something?" he asked. I exaggerated thinking about it and then nodded.

"What do you want to watch?" I asked.

"I don't know... something stupid or sad." He took a minute to think. "From the nineties..." he thought harder, "Oh, 'The Secret Garden'!" I rolled my eyes and walked over to his vast movie collection and easily found the movie.

"Really?" I asked incredulous.

"Oh, don't even act like it's not the best." he said. I laughed and put it in the DVD player. I laid down next to him and he pulled me in closer. I don't know where I would be without him, and I worried that this road I was on with Nick and Jack would ruin our friendship. I had lied to Matt. I had no idea how to fix any of this.

$$$

I spent the remainder of my weekend taking care of Nick. I parked on the street a few blocks down from Bingos. Nick lived in a split level house that had been converted into apartments. I looked for his name on the mailboxes before choosing the door on the right. Pushing the doorbell I waited for him to answer noticing the peeling paint on the white siding. The door opened and I gasped. Nicks bruises had set in and he looked worse than he did at the hospital. I couldn't stop myself from hugging him, he winced.

"Sorry," I said unwrapping myself. He pulled me back into his arms, before I got too far away.

"It's not as bad as it looks," he said, stepping aside so I could enter. Nick's home looked a bit like a frat house. Immediately to my left was a large TV surrounded by a worn out couch and two hideously green chairs. Behind them I could see the kitchen with a beer pong table situated in the middle. A hallway separated the two and I could only assume the bedrooms were down it.

"You look like you've been hit by a car," I said.

"What, you don't find this ruggedly handsome?" he asked motioning at himself with his good arm. "I'm honestly surprised you aren't already naked lying in my bed." He laughed and then sharply inhaled a breath while holding his side. I flushed red all over and quickly averted my eyes as Nick stared down at me for a little too long. "I love teasing you," he said.

"Because it's so easy?" I asked.

"No, because I've never seen anyone look more beautiful in red."

I stayed with Nick that night. We fell asleep talking and watching old movies on TCM.

A loud banging woke us up the next morning and we both walked out of the bedroom to see what it was. Ben and Max were carrying a large box of groceries. Multiple packs of beer were scattered trailing from the front door to the kitchen. Noticing us, the boys dropped the box.

"Finally! Now that you've boned, maybe Nick will stop moping around like a love sick pussy," Max said. Ben threw a dish towel at him.

"Get to work, master chef," Ben said to Max.

"What's going on?" I asked looking at Ben pulling various things from the box.

"Friendsgiving," Nick said behind me.

"You should come," Ben added.

"Yes, you should come," Nick said wrapping his arms around my waist and resting his chin on my shoulder.

"I'd have to go home and change," I said leaning

my head back. Ben poured some coffee into a travel mug he retrieved from one of the cabinets.

"Here. For the road," he said handing it to me.

"Thanks." I took the mug and started to grab my stuff.

"Whoa, you don't have to leave now. Friendsgiving won't start till much later," Nick said.

"Yea, but I have to run some errands and do laundry. I promise I will be quick." Nick walked toward me handing me my jacket. Kissing me lightly we walked to the door. Before leaving I heard a sharp slap and Nick yell at Max.

"Don't talk like that to my girl!"

$$$

I don't think I've ever dressed faster. I should have just stayed and showered at Nick's, because it took me longer to drive back to his house, thanks to traffic, than it did to shower, dress, do laundry, and shop for groceries. When I eventually arrived there were a handful of cars parked along Nick's block. Finally finding a spot to park, I timidly walked up the steps. I could hear a lot of voices coming through the door as I knocked.

"It's open," someone yelled from the inside. I turned the knob and took a deep breath before walking in. There were a lot more people than when I had left. The boys had turned the couch around to rest nearer to the table. The ugly green chairs anchored the couch and random stools were scattered around the empty side. The table was decked out with a turkey and all the fixings. Who knew Max could cook? I stepped into the room where Ben and Max chatted with a couple of dudes while a few girls hovered near the fridge, arms wrapped around their beaus. Nick sat on one of the stools wiping mashed potatoes on a very cute brunette. A pang of jealousy surged through me. *Who was this bitch all up on my man?* I thought, going a little bit gangster for a second. My jealousy didn't last long. Once Nick realized it was me, he left the bimbo's side.

"Hey babe you look great!" he said wrapping me up into a hug. He led me into the group introducing me to the people around the room before returning us to the table.

"…and this is Kate. She works day shift at the bar," he said. I extended my hand to Kate while simultaneously leaning into Nick a little more than I would normally. *He's mine bitch.*

"Hi, it's nice to finally meet you!" Kate said. Oh great she's nice.

"Yea, it's nice to meet you, too," I said trying to kill her with kindness.

"Can I get you ladies something to drink?" Nick asked.

"Yea, I'll have another." Kate said.

"I'll have the same." I said. I didn't know what she was drinking, but I didn't care. I was beginning to feel really awkwad crashing Nick's Friendsgiving.

"Are you sure?" Nick leaned down to whisper in my ear. "You know how strong Max mixes the drinks, and that's a premade Long Island." I didn't want to look weak in front of Nick and his friends, I also didn't want Nick to get in the habit of worrying every time I drank. I would sip this one slowly.

"I can handle it," I said giving him my most reassuring smile. Nick nodded and walked away toward the bar. Kate smiled at me, and the silence grew in length as I tried to think of something to say. Kate squirmed before clearing her throat.

"This is going to sound weird and I'm really not trying to be out of line here, but you're dating Nick..." I nodded and waited for her to tell me whatever it was that would offend me. "You're taking this seriously right? With Nick? I mean he's still pretty fragile, and I just, I just..." I held up my hand to stop her. Who the hell did she think she was? Of course I was serious about Nick. Why would she ask that? I worried briefly that she knew something about Jack, but how could she? She was clearly interested in Nick, and one thing was certain, I needed to nip this in the bud.

"This really isn't any of your business, but I wouldn't be here if I wasn't serious about Nick. Now do I need to be worried about you getting too serious with my boyfriend?" I said. *Wow where did that come from?*

"Oh no! We are just friends." She said holding her hands up in surrender. I narrowed my eyes at her in warning. "I'm so..." she didn't have time to finish before Nick came back with our drinks.

"Thanks." I said taking mine. I took a larger drink than I intended while I was still eyeing Kate. The liquor burned my mouth and throat. I would have to drink this very, very slowly.

"Are you fucks ready?" Max yelled carrying

another bowl of stuffing. Everyone gathered around the table and sat. Nick sat to my left and Ben to my right. Like a silent bell had chimed to signify the beginning of mass everyone joined hands with the people next to them. Max cleared his throat. "Dear Jesus, or God, or Alien, or whatever divine being lives in the sky and messes around with our lives... Thank you. Amen." Nick and Ben squeezed my hands before letting go. Together we ate and I talked with Ben about the new beers the bar was getting on tap. We were interrupted by Max who seemed to be acting as the master of ceremony for the event.

"Ok, so let's go around and say what we're thankful for. Nick you start." He looked at Nick.

"I am thankful that I have a great group of friends, that I haven't fallen into old habits, and that everyone I know is relatively healthy and happy." He looked at me meaningfully. *If only he knew,* I thought. Everyone's eyes settled on me and I looked at my plate.

"I am thankful for all of the people I have met this year," I said. *Well most of them*, I thought. It was Ben's turn now.

"I am thankful for stuffing." He said deadpan. Everyone laughed, and eventually the line of thanks landed back on Max.

"I am thankful for girls...and daddy issues," he said grinning from ear to ear. Everyone groaned and Nick threw a handful of green beans at him. The room erupted into a massive food fight. Peas, mashed potatoes, and a turkey leg flew through the air as Nick dragged me under the table.

"I'm thankful for you," he said wiping yams from my face and kissing me softly.

CHAPTER TWENTY-SEVEN

I kissed Nick goodbye Tuesday morning. He had a flight to catch and I had work to get to.

"You could stay another hour," he said wrapping his arms around me.

"I can't. I have to work," I said kissing his cheek. Our nights had stayed pretty PG-13 which I had mixed emotions about. On one hand I wanted to move our physical relationship forward. On the other hand I had Jack and he held my virginity secured snuggly in his bill fold.

"Fine, but before you leave I need to ask you a question," he said. I nodded wondering what he could possibly want to know. "What are you doing next Wednesday night?" he asked.

"I have to work, but I could probably move things around... why what did you have in mind?" I snuggled closer to him.

"It's my mom's birthday, and I thought you might like to come to dinner." I stiffened in his arms. "I would really like you to meet my family," he finished. *That's a major step*, I thought. Especially because he had just reconnected with them himself. What if he expects to meet my family now? There is no way he can meet my mom, I wasn't ready for that. I cared for Nick though and I could see in his eyes how much he wanted me to be there. I had called off work Monday and we had been inseparable all weekend. I didn't know if it was love or not, it didn't feel like what I imagined love would feel like, but I felt something as I looked into his passionate green eyes.

"Yea, I'll be there," I said. I couldn't say no to meeting his family, but I would be lying if I said I was looking forward to it. What if his mom could sense that I was lying...well not lying, but withholding valuable information from him. What if she could like smell Jack on me or see the guilt dripping all over my face. Nick squeezed me noticing my worried expression. I quickly gave him a reassuring smile as I hugged him one last time before letting go. I walked to my car while Nick stood watching me leave. I threw my bag into the trunk, but not before pulling my long since dead cell phone from it. I plugged it into the car charger, waiting for the telltale beep to indicate it was charging, before pulling out onto the street waving to Nick one last time before I drove away. What was I doing? It was way too early to start meeting parents! I had just met and hopefully appeased the friends. My phone pinged as I stopped at a red light. I opened the message from Nick.

I know I should have told you
this in person, but I think I might
be falling in love with you.
– Nick

The light turned green and I pulled forward not responding to his message. What was I supposed to say? My phone rang and I ignored it without looking at the screen. It was probably Nick with texters remorse. My phone rang again, annoyed, I picked it up. It was Matt. I accepted the call, put it on speaker phone, and rested the phone on my boobs.

"Hey Matt, I'm on my way in. Want me to pick up some breakfast, or lunch?" I asked noticing it was closer to eleven than it was to ten.

"Hey, change of plans. Jack wants you to see him," Matt said trying to keep his cool. I could tell he was nervous again.

"Okay, sure what time?" I asked feeling more confident with every turn. I could do this. I could juggle Nick, while fulfilling my obligation to Jack, and also manage Matt's freak outs.

"Um, right fucking now!" Matt said losing a bit of his composure.

"Now?" I asked. Why the hell did Jack need me there right now? He was still at work. What was he going to do, bend me over his desk.

"Yes! Now! He said that you weren't able to make one of your dates," he said dates like it left a sour taste in his mouth. "He's just checking in on his long term investment." He said it like I was an office chair being shipped from China, every syllable of the sentence burned into me as I realized how insignificant I was to Jack in the scheme of things. He was a major player at a multibillion dollar company, and I was just his latest toy.

"Okay don't freak out, I'll head that way," I said turning back towards downtown.

"Of course you know where he works." Matt somehow managed to yell and sigh at the same time.

"Yea, I took him a package when you were out of town. I thought it was part of my to-do list," I said not wanting to deal with Matt's whiney shit anymore. Matt sighed.

"It wasn't," he said. "But you know what is on your to-do list? Jack. Jack is on your to-do list. He's not on your to-date list! He is on your to-do list meaning your should do him... now!" I was stunned into silence. My face burned with embarrassment. "I'm sorry but, please, please don't fuck this up. This business isn't sustainable without Jack. Do you understand?" What does that mean? I thought Jack was just the money behind all the fancy clothes and dinners. Did he play a bigger role than I thought?

"Ginny, do you hear me?" Matt's tone had intensified.

"Yea! I hear you!" I said before Matt ended the call. What the hell have I gotten myself into?

$$$

I walked down the cold stark hall of Miller Cove Financial, and knocked on Jack's office door.

"Come in." Melissa called through the door.

"Hello again, Vivie." She said as I entered the office. "Jack is expecting you, go on in." I lightly wrapped on the door behind Melissa's desk.

"Come in," Jack said. I pushed open the heavy door and walked in. Closing it before looking at Jack. He was sitting behind his desk staring intently at his computer. He hadn't even noticed that it was me who had entered. A small smile lit my face as I stared at him working. He looked so at home in his office, so strong and confident...and sexy as hell.

"One second, I will be right with you," he said still not looking up from his computer. Not wanting to sit, I walked around his office looking at the books and pictures he kept on his shelves. I paused on one of him posing with an older blond woman in a sharp blue suit. I felt him behind me before he had a chance to speak.

"Is this your mom?" I asked. Looking at the picture I noticed her eyes. They were sharper than Jack's, and held flecks of his intense green.

"Yes, that was the day I graduated from college. The day I started working here," he said as I turned toward him.

"Sorry I left you at the hotel. I should have left a note or something." I said. Jack led me to one of the chairs in front of his desk; he took the other.

"It was fine, the date was over," he said.

"Then why all the theatrics with Matt?" I asked.

"Honestly, I thought you were running. You were gone from the hotel when I woke up, and then you didn't answer any of my emails concerning this Thursday," he said staring at me. "I called Matt as a last ditch effort." He shrugged. "I may have gone a little hard on him."

"Ya think?" I laughed. "I think we are giving him an aneurism." Jack laughed briefly before his eyes turned serious.

"Spend the day with me." He said it like a command, but his eyes were asking me.

"Doing what? Sitting here while you con kids out of all of their money?" I asked. Jack frowned and I could feel the cold wall building back up between us. "I'm sorry, Jack," I sighed. A part of me wanted to be with him. "Of course I will spend the day with you, whatever you want." Sometimes he acted like a petulant child, but we fit together so well. I was in the pit of the devil's lair and I felt more comfortable with him here than I did in my own apartment...or even Nick's apartment. Melissa's voice came over the intercom.

"Mr. Eagle, the conference room is ready for your video call with Mrs. Landerman in fifteen." Melissa said clearly before I heard the distinct click of her call end.

"Thank you, Melissa," Jack said holding down a button while he spoke. He rubbed his hands through his hair and over his face before turning back to face me. "I can't miss this call," he said.

"I can wait."

"It's going to last a few hours," he said sullenly.

"Maybe next time?" I asked as I stood and walked toward the door.

"Tuesday," he said to my back. "Have dinner with me." I turned to face him. I smiled excited at the prospect of seeing him again, realizing at the same time that that I was depressed we wouldn't be spending the day together.

"When? Where?" I said turning back to the door.

"Six, I'll pick you up at six."

"We have a deal, Mr. Eagle," I said turning to get one more look at him before leaving. He was smiling at me when I walked out of the door. The second I passed Melissa on my way out of the building the haze fell from my eyes and I remembered Nick. Why did I have so much fun with Jack? Even when we did nothing I still had the time of my life. There was an excitement and equally a calmness that surrounded him. When we were together I could forget about the money and the sex, but as soon as I left him it all came back into view.

CHAPTER TWENTY-EIGHT

"Mom, I'm home," I said dropping my bag by the door and walking through our tiny living room.

"Hi, Sweetie. I'm in the kitchen!" Mary Allen said. I couldn't help but smile at the image of my mom standing over boiling pots in a yellow and white flowered apron. "Dinner's almost ready. How was the drive?" she asked turning to look at me.

"Good. You've lost weight." I said hugging her slight frame.

"Really? I've been eating like a horse!" she said holding me at arm's length and looking me over. The boiling water spilled over the pot's edge causing the flame on the gas stove to flicker. She turned back to the appliance.

"Grab some plates. Dinner is two minutes away."

We ate and talked about what I had been up to. I told her about the new job and dodged her questions about who I was dating.

"So how have the meetings been going?" I

asked. The last time I had talked to her she had been going to her AA meetings religiously.

"Fine, fine let's not talk about bad things while you're here. I'm fine," she said.

"It's not a bad thing, Mom! It's really good, I'm proud of you for sticking with it."

"I'm more proud of you," she said, "So what are your plans for tonight? You and Hailey going to hang out with the old gang?" I didn't have the heart to tell her about the letter from Miller Cover, and the delicate balancing act I was doing in order to get my degree.

"Yea, I think I'm gonna go hang out with Maggie for a bit." She nodded grabbing my plate before she stood. I couldn't tell her that Hailey and I weren't friends anymore. She wouldn't have let it go without an explanation and I couldn't tell her about Hailey and Derek.

"I can get that Mom. You cooked, I'll clean," I said standing.

"No, no I've got it, sweetie." She kissed me on the head. "You go get ready for your night out." I ignored her and grabbed the remaining bowls and walked into the kitchen passing the fridge where a list of emergency numbers was hanging. I set the bowls on the counter.

"I love you, Mom. Thanks for dinner."

"I love you too, Baby." She filled the sink with soapy water. I started walking out of the room, but paused watching her for a minute before heading to the bathroom. She did look better.

$$$

Maggie and I met in the parking lot of the bar. As we entered I recognized a ton of people from our small town all sitting around tiny square tables. Walking up to the counter we waited for the bartender to finish with his current clients before getting to us. We waved hello to some familiar faces we hadn't seen in awhile and chatted with old classmates who's names escaped us.

"I've already got us pitchers." said Murphy slinging his arms around us and pulling us in for a hug. After embracing we followed him back to the booth where Jeff was guarding the drinks.

"Where's Grace?" Maggie asked Murphy as we all settled into the booth. I waved at Jeff, Murphy's best friend since high school, and accepted the glass he handed me.

"She's visiting with her family tonight," he said. I remembered meeting Murphy's wife, Grace, briefly before they got married. Murphy looked at Jeff before turning back toward us. "She can't drink." he said.

"Oh my God!" Maggie yelled. I didn't know Grace very well, but Maggie was better at keeping in contact with people than I was. "Are you going to be a daddy?" Murphy smiled and nodded. The table exploded in congratulations. Maggie and I turned to each other and started mimicking how Murphy would be as a father.

"If you don't cut it out I will pour this beer over your head!" he threatened laughing and holding his solo cup up.

"Seriously though Murph, congrats!" I said. We

continued to catch up until the music got so loud we couldn't hear each other. Succumbing to the throbbing beat we joined the other locals out on the dance floor. I was feeling pretty good, not drunk, but a strong buzz. Murphy and Jeff took turns spinning us around and before we knew it half of the patrons had left the bar. I got out my phone to see what time it was and noticed I had a missed call from Jack.

"I'm going to use the bathroom." I mouthed at Murphy before heading toward the back hall. Pushing open the family bathroom I closed the door and dialed Jack's number.

"Hello, Vivie, are you ok?" Jack answered.

"Yea, I'm like totally good! How are you?" I turned toward the mirror making faces at myself.

"Are you drunk?" he asked.

"No, I'm not drunk, I am very, very tipsy," I said setting the phone on speaker and placing it on the side of the sink. I started pulling my hair out of its pony tail and readjusting it.

"Where are you?"

"I'm at home. I'm fine I just saw that I missed a call from you and wanted to see what's up," I said smoothing out my bleeding eye liner.

"Where at home?"

"Jack, I'm," I stopped seeing the door to the bathroom open. I stalled my mind momentarily flashing back to Molvak and the ruined dinner. The intruder entered and I screamed.

"No! No! Get away!" Murphy, Jeff, and Maggie had all busted into the bathroom with half filled cups. They were all wet and smelled like the floor at a brewery. Before I could get away Murphy poured his over my head.

"Welcome Home!" he said pulling me into a wet smelly group hug.

"You guys are awful!" I said wiping my wet head on Maggie's arms.

"Guys, guys, guys," Jeff said, "we have a casualty!" he yelled dropping to his knees in front of the toilet and pulling my phone from the bowl with his index and middle finger. It was soaked and Jack was no longer on the other end. Whoops.

"NOOOOOOO!" Murphy yelled also dropping to his knees while staring at the ceiling.

"Gross, I'll see if the bartender has any rice." Maggie laughed, grabbing the phone with a wad of toilet paper and heading out of the bathroom.

An hour later we sat finishing our beers. I had my phone securely zipped inside a ziploc bag of rice by my feet.

"That's it for us guys," Murphy said draining his beer. "I've got to get home to the wife."

"Yea, I should probably go too," Maggie said. We all hugged and said our goodbyes walking outside.

"Shit, I forgot my rice." I said. Murphy and Jeff were already heading down the street out of ear shot.

"Want me to wait for you?" Maggie asked rubbing her eyes smearing makeup all over her face.

"No, it's fine, dude," I said hugging her one last time. "Call me sometime. Let's make this like a regular thing."

"I'd like that," Maggie said, getting into her car.

I ran back into the bar waving at the bartender. They had to be closing soon, even though there were still a few people drinking. I slid into the table and reached down for the bag of rice. Finally finding it, I sat back up just in time to see Jack Eagle burst through the doors.

CHAPTER TWENTY-NINE

Our eyes locked and he ran toward me. When I say Jack ran I mean he walked with great force.

"Are you ok? What happened?" he said as I stood up clutching the bag of rice to my chest.

"What?" I didn't know what to say. "What are you doing here, Jack?" the next song started making talking almost impossible. Jack tried to say something but I couldn't understand. I stepped closer to hear him. His smell encased me and I closed my eyes as I felt his breath on my ear.

"I was worried, I thought something happened to you. I heard you scream and I thought..." he paused. I stepped a little closer.

"What did you think?" I asked.

"I thought back to the night we first met, when I heard you screaming from the bathroom." A sad smile came to my face as I remembered Jack pulling Molvak off of me. The way his green eyes flashed dangerously as he told me to run.

"It was just some friends playing a joke. I'm sorry I didn't mean to worry you."

"I tried to call you back, but you didn't answer." I raised the bag of rice.

"My phone fell in the toilet." I laughed. "How did you find me?" Jack looked nervous pulling away from me. Holding me at arms length he let his eyes travel down my body. The song stopped and before another started Jack, melancholy, looked at me.

"You're really ok?" he asked. That look would haunt me for the rest of my life. That moment burned into my brain. The second I realized this wasn't just about the sex or the money. Jack had to have some sort of feelings for me, and I couldn't deny that I was happy he was here. The next song started, it was slower and all I wanted was for Jack to stay.

"Dance with me," I said. He didn't hear me over the music, so I set the rice on the table and moved my hands to his shoulders stepping closer to him. "Dance with me," I repeated. He hesitated before pulling me onto the dance floor. We didn't talk, we just danced. Our bodies moving together like they were always meant to be as one. Eventually the music ended and the bartender made the last call.

"Let me drive you home," Jack said pulling away.

"My car is here," I said picking up the bag of rice.

"You can take my car, I will drive yours. I haven't been drinking," he said scolding me with his eyes for even thinking about driving. "Just give my driver your address and I will follow you," he said sticking his hand out for my keys. I rummaged in my coat pocket and handed them over.

Jack's driver opened the door to the car for me and I gave him my address. Sliding into the spacious town car I couldn't help but notice the butterflies in my stomach.

"I'm glad we found you, Ms. Vivie," the driver said.

"How did you find me?" I asked before I could stop myself. "Sorry, I don't even know your name."

"It's Henry, Ms.," he answered pulling onto the street. "Mr. Eagle knew you were coming home... there aren't a lot of bars in this town." He laughed.

"You went to all the bars?" I asked shocked. He was right, there weren't that many, only about a dozen, but still.

"No, no don't worry about that, this was only number six," he said still chuckling while I sat in stunned silence.

"How long have you been working for Jack?" I asked. Henry appeared to be in his early fifties. He wore a black suit with a black tie. His dark brown hair was spattered with grey patches around his temples.

"Oh, I've been working for Mr. Eagle since he was five." Henry laughed his big laugh again as we pulled onto my block. "He's very fond of you," he said looking at me sincerely. There was something else in his eyes too. Maybe a warning? I didn't have time to speculate before we pulled up to my house and Henry exited the car to appear at my door. "It was nice to finally meet you, Ms. Vivie," he said tipping his head as Jack pulled up and exited my car.

"You too, Henry, I hope we meet again," I said knowing that after next week we wouldn't...unless...unless maybe I felt something more for Jack, and if he felt more for me too. "Thank you for your help, Jack," I said, turning to walk up the steps to my house.

"Let me walk you in," he said taking my hand.

"It's ok I've," I stopped. The door was halfway open and I could see glass winking up at me from just inside. Jack followed my eyes and saw the mess.

"Stay here," he said going to the open door. I didn't listen and followed. He bent down. "It's a liquor bottle," he said pushing the door open wider, holding up the shredded remains of what was once a bottle of Vodka.

"Mom?" I said pushing past him.

"Vivie, no!" he said but it didn't matter. I was already in. The house was dark, but I could hear movement in the kitchen. I stumbled over random furniture that was in my way while I ran toward the sound.

"Mom?" I yelled again moving around the island. A dark shape was visible on the ground. As I got closer I realized it was her, I knelt down beside her. "Mom, what happened?" I asked rubbing her back and arms not knowing what to do. The light flickered on and I noticed the blood pooling around her hand. I rolled her over. She instinctively moved to shield her eyes from the light; the only damage was the cut to her hand.

"Genevieve Madison Allen!" she tried to yell, but her voice came out raw. "What on earth are you doing up at this hour? Go to bed right now or no cartoons!"

"Mom you're cut! What happened?"

Rolling back onto her stomach she mumbled, "Go back to bed and maybe I'll make you pancakes in the morning." She closed her eyes, but before she had a chance to fall back asleep she threw up all over herself and the floor.

"Mom!" I shook her again tears falling down my face. I heard the sirens coming down the street. I hadn't even heard Jack call 911. "I...I don't know what happened," I said more to myself than to Jack.

"She drank too much," Jack said looking into a paper bag sitting on the counter. He reached in, the clinking of bottles giving away what was inside, and pulled out a receipt. "There are three bottles still in here and it looks like she bought," he paused scanning the receipt, "Six," he finished. Henry showed the paramedics in and I moved out of their way. Jack explained his theory to them and they put her on the gurney. When they left I followed jumping into the back of the ambulance with them. The last thing I saw as we pulled away was Jack standing in my mother's doorway.

CHAPTER THIRTY

"Are you sure you don't want me to walk you in?" Murphy asked as we pulled up in front of the dark house. Jack's car was gone. What had I dragged him into? It was stupid, but a part of me was sad he hadn't stayed. I wanted him there. He knew what it was like to have a parent who was...damaged. I turned toward Murphy. He looked so big crammed into his tiny car. His bushy brown beard contrasted nicely with his soft blue eyes. It would be so easy to ask him to stay, but he had a wife and a family to get back to. I was happy for him, but also insanely jealous. I wanted that; the love, the companionship, the security.

"No, Murphy, I'm fine. Thank you for picking me up," I said leaning in for a hug. Murphy wrapped me in his big strong arms. I could feel the tears preparing to fall. I pushed them down and pulled away.

"You can always talk to me, Ginny, about

anything," he said. I turned my head and opened the door. I knew if he saw me crying he would never leave and that wasn't fair to his family. I couldn't pretend to be loved, and I needed to stop pretending that everything was alright.

"Thanks again, Murph," I said turning to go. Trudging up the steps to the house, I unlocked the door and walked in. I let the tears fall down my face. *Alone*, I thought. I let the anger and fear and disappointment cover and flow around me. She had been sober, or so I thought. All the money and worry I'd spent on her disease was worth it when she was sober. Was it seeing me that triggered it again? I had lied and told her everything was fine, that I was fine. I didn't realize that she would take it to mean that I was fine away from her; fine without her. What was the alternative though? Telling her the truth? Had the relapse been coming for awhile? That seemed impossible but it was the only reason I could come up with.

The table next to the door was covered in photographs of the two of us at different stages in our lives. I clenched my fists as I looked at our smiling faces. There was the one where we were at the park for my seventh birthday. Derrick had been strategically cut out of the picture. That photo was followed by a series of memories from when I was twelve, fifteen, and when I graduated high school. There were no recent pictures no pictures from before Derrick had entered our lives or after he had left. I threw my hands across the table smashing all of the frames to the floor. Screaming I watched the happy faces crack and splinter. I fell to the ground and hit my fists against the wood. Slumping my shoulders, I sat there crying. I heard the floor boards creak and looked up. Maybe it was a burglar, I didn't care, but it wasn't a burglar. It was Jack.

"Hey," I said wiping my face with the back of my hand.

"You're bleeding," he said stepping forward.

"I tripped," I said starting to pick up the pieces of broken glass scattered on the floor. Jack knelt down and started gathering glass.

"I used to trip a lot," he said. I clenched the glass shards in my hands. I didn't want him to see me like this.

"What are you doing here? This isn't a date, Jack. This is life, my life! What am I going to owe you for this display of fake affection? A blowy in your office? Or do you want instant gratification? I could do a little dance for you right now!"

"Stop!" Jack yelled. When I didn't he wrapped his hands around my wrists and squeezed until the pain was too much and I let the glass fall to the floor. Tiny pieces stuck to the blood on my hands.

He stood and pulled me up with him still holding my wrists. He walked toward the hallway leading to the bedrooms.

"Let go of me!" I said pulling my hands free.

"What are you doing?" he tried to grab me again but I wiggled away. "Stop it, Vivie!" He caught me, wrapping his arms around my body so my hands were trapped down at my sides. He picked me up like that and started walking down the hallway.

"Jack this is ridiculous!" I said squirming.

"Then stop acting like a child!" he yelled back.

The light was on in the bathroom and he set me on the ground. Putting down the lid on the toilet, "Sit!" he ordered. I refused.

"Why are you here?" I asked.

"Sit down so I can take care of your hands."

"Why are you here, Jack?" I asked again.

"You know why I'm here. Sit!" I stayed where I was.

"No, I don't. Tell me why you're here."

"God damn it, Vivie, sit down so I can take care of you!"

"No! Tell me!" we were so close, but yelling like we were a million miles away from each other.

"I want you!" he said. Disgusted I tried to push past him. Why had I thought it was anything more than sex and money. This was all part of his ploy to get me to trust him. I was an idiot for thinking there might actually be something here. Why couldn't Nick have the power to draw me in like Jack? He stopped me from leaving and I threw my hands up in the air. I didn't care about the three date rule; I pushed all feelings for Jack aside as I unbuttoned my pants.

"What are you doing?" he whispered.

"I can't do this anymore Jack!" I said. "I need this to be over. You're…you're driving me insane. I thought, I don't know what I thought, and it doesn't matter. You want me and I want out. I want to forget this ever happened." I dropped my pants to the floor and walked over to him. He was standing still as a statue. I moved to the sink turning it on and rinsing the blood from my hands. This was always how this was going to end. I was a fool for thinking it would be some kind of beautiful union. I knew there wouldn't be love, but I hoped there would at least be like. Now I hated him; the kind of hate that twists and rots in your gut. I dried my hands. Jack hadn't moved, he stared at me like I was a wild creature, and I had to admit I felt like one. A scared tiger backed into a corner with no way out. I walked over to him and pulled down his tie. Letting it fall to the floor, I started unbuttoning his shirt. He moved his hands over mine.

"Vivie..." he whispered. His breathing had picked up, his mouth slightly open.

"It's never been real, Jack. All we've ever done is pretend," I said freeing my hands to continue their work.

"I wasn't," he said. I laughed a little pulling his shirt off his shoulders and letting it join his tie. "What?" he asked.

"Nothing," I said looking down. Jack lifted his hands to my face pulling my head up to meet his eyes. "You're right. You never let on that it was anything more than money for sex." I said unbuckling his pants.

"How can you be so stupid?" he asked backing away from me.

Glaring at him as he ran his hands through his hair I yelled, "I'm not stupid! I'm naïve remember?" I reached for the undone belt and pulled it from the loops. He stepped closer putting his hands on my shoulders.

"I said I didn't want you to pretend, I want the real Vivie, I want you to trust me."

The tears welled and spilled over my eyes before

I could stop them. I pushed on his chest but he held me where I was.

"This isn't pretend, Jack! I trust you more than anyone else in the entire world. Which really says something about me since I know that you're going to break my heart. The anticipation of losing you next week is killing me! You are breaking me!" I shouted. "So let's just get it over with!"

"I don't want to get it over with!" he shouted. "I want a thousand more dates. I can't get anything done anymore, I go to work and you're all I think about. I just sit there at my desk and try to think of ways I can prolong this. When you aren't with me I wonder who you are with and if they could possibly care about you as much as I do! I can't stand the thought of making love to you and you going back into the arms of your boyfriend. I fell in love with you the moment I saw you!"

I couldn't think. Jack loved me. Jack wanted me. Not just my body, but everything. I pulled him close and kissed him hard. He pushed me away.

"Do you love me?" he asked. The world dropped away and I imagined our lives together. Did I love Jack? The immoral part of my brain screamed yes! If Jack and I worked, I would never have to worry about money again. I still had the letter from Miller Cove in my backpack; the letter stating that all of my loans had been paid. The only person who could have done that was Jack. I waited for the moral side of my brain to kick in but it was too busy categorizing every surface of Jack's face as he stared intently at me. I realized then it didn't matter if Jack was the wrong choice, it didn't matter that

Nick was strong and stable, I wanted Jack. I wanted all of his crazy shit and mood changes, because it all came with an open honest person. I would never be able to open up to Nick the way I had opened up to Jack. I looked into his dark green eyes and nodded. He gripped me a little tighter.

"Say it," he said.

"I love you, too," I expected a long lingering kiss that would lead us into the bedroom where I could finally be with him. I did not expect him to pull out his phone and hand it to me.

"Call him, end it," he said. I blinked a few times in confusion.

"What?" I asked.

"Call what's his name, your boyfriend...end it."

"Jack, it's the middle of the night. Plus I can't do it over the phone." I said thinking, *Why can't he just shut up and kiss me?*

"You. Are. Killing. Me." He said running his hands through his hair and pulling. Well this was a one-eighty.

"What's the problem? I'm seeing him on Wednesday. I'll do it then." I said. Nick wouldn't be back till Tuesday. I owed it to him to break it off face to face, plus if I tried doing it over the phone he wouldn't accept it. He could be a little persistent.

"Not good enough," he said. "I want you now!"

"I want you now too. What's the big deal? You were going to sleep with me before!" I knew that sounded bad and I knew tomorrow I would feel guilty about what I was doing behind Nick's back, but right now all I cared about was being with Jack. There had never been passion with Nick like there was with Jack. I loved Jack with an urgency, because I didn't know how long I would get to keep him.

"We don't know that," Jack said. "I won't share, Vivie. When we're together I want us to be wholly together." He ran his hands up and down my arms. I was frustrated and his movements only stoked the anger. I pushed the phone back into his hand.

"Then I guess we'll have to wait until Thursday." I said sternly. His face fell. Why did he have to be so pushy? I was his, he had me, he won, but that wasn't good enough and although I wanted nothing more than to be his, I couldn't make myself call Nick. He deserved better than me, and I deserved to watch as I broke his heart.

"It will be one hell of a third date," he said.

CHAPTER THIRTY-ONE

I walked into my apartment Sunday morning and didn't feel the usual depression waft over me. The holiday weekend hadn't gone as planned. No, in fact it was a complete shit storm. Jack had arranged for my mother to go to the same treatment facility that his mother had gone too, and I cried when I left her. She avoided me for the most part until eventually refusing to see me at all. She was ashamed of herself, and a tiny part of me was ashamed of her too. Jack stayed with me until I left. He made a point not to touch me. I understood, but either way I couldn't end it with Nick that way. The part of me that wanted to do nothing more than lock myself away with Jack was screaming to be unleashed while the other half was enjoying watching Jack's plan backfire. He had moped around when he wasn't busy arranging things. Jack was mine and all I had to do was wait a few more days till I could be his.

$$$

Monday morning a call woke me up. With my eyes still closed I reached over to the night stand feeling for my phone.

"Hello," I said with a gravelly voice, I cleared it.

"Hey babe, how was Thanksgiving?" Nick asked. Oh No! Why hadn't I thought he would call me? I started shaking and sat up, looking around like he was going to pop out from around the corner. Seeing that the room was empty I answered.

"Hey, how's Georgia?"

"Good, I love visiting my dad, but I miss you!" he said. I wanted to have missed him the way that he missed me, but I couldn't. I was Jack's completely. My stomach turned as I realized that Nick and I might not be friends by the end of the week. He might hate me by then, and I might not blame him. Nick was one of my best friends. How much would that change?

"Mine was fine," I said, trying not to lead him on while simultaneously leading him on and lying. I knew it was selfish but I couldn't let him go yet.

"Good, so I have some bad news," he paused. "Well you've probably already guessed it," he laughed. Guessed what? Maybe he was moving to Georgia full time, or any other reason that would make it redundant to have to totally crush him after meeting his parents.

"I haven't the slightest," I said crossing my fingers.

"My flight's been pushed back to Wednesday

due to the storm. Has it hit yet?" he asked. I got up and opened my curtains. The light momentarily blinded me.

"Holy hell!" I said into the phone. Thick white flakes fell in large clumps from the sky. The streets were already covered.

"I'll take that as a yes," Nick laughed. "The news is showing people abandoning their cars on Lakeshore."

"I...I need to call my boss," I said looking at the clock, I knew I wasn't expected for another three hours, but there was no way I could make it in this.

"Okay, will you still be able to meet me at the airport?" he asked.

"Yea, are you sure you're gonna make it to the airport?" I laughed.

"Come hell or high snow," he said. I groaned at his bad joke. "Alright I'll let you get back to work."

"Okay email me your flight info."

"Will do, love you." He paused. I didn't know if he meant to say it or if it just came out. Either way I couldn't say it back.

"See you Wednesday, bye." I hung up the phone. I laid back down on the bed. This whole breaking up thing was going to be harder than I thought. My phone rang in my hand. It was Matt.

"Hello."

"Hey wanna go sledding?" Matt asked.

"You're insane," I yawned.

"That's why you love me." Why was everyone so into love this week? "Needless to say work is cancelled...I could email you some stuff today to work on, but I just said work was cancelled."

"Okay boss man...when do you want me to come back?"

"I don't know, I'd guess the streets should be good by Wednesday, but let's play it by ear," he said. "Maybe Friday?"

"Jesus you're such a slave driver!" We both laughed.

"I'm already bored," he said.

"I'm still in bed," I countered.

"Wanna watch a movie?" he asked.

"How?" I laughed. "I'm not driving in this and neither are you!"

"What movies do you have?" he asked.

"Oh, let's see, I have about four." I walked out of my bedroom and down the hall. Stooping in front of the entertainment center I pulled out the only DVD's I had.

"Okay, we have *The Notebook*..."

"No," he interrupted.

"Will you let me say the names before you object?" I complained.

"Fine, sorry," he apologized.

"Okay, thank you, like I said before, *The Notebook, The Last Unicorn, Labyrinth*, and *Goonies*," I finished.

"Those are fucking random movies," he laughed. "How about *Labyrinth*? David Bowie gives me a boner."

"Me too." I laughed taking the movie out of the case and putting it in the DVD player. I waited for the menu to come up.

"Okay," Matt said. "On the count of three push play. One...Two...Three..."

$$$

I turned off the DVD player and stretched.

"I just… I love it so much," I said. Matt didn't respond. "Matt?" I could hear his deep breathing through the phone. "Night, Matt." I ended the call and walked over to the kitchen. I was starving, but opening the fridge only revealed some juice, butter, and a bag of dark chocolate bars. The doorbell rang and I ran to answer it. Looking through the peephole I couldn't help but smile, and then immediately frown. I hadn't showered, I was still in my pajamas and my hair was piled on top of my head. There was no way I was going to let Jack in looking like this.

"What are you doing here?" I asked.

"You didn't answer your phone," he said through the door.

"That's not an answer," I said.

"I was worried, I brought food." My stomach growled. "Traitor" I said to it.

"What?" he asked.

"Nothing, I'm not dressed."

"You're rarely dressed around me," he laughed.

"Not true!" I said.

"Absolutely true." He laughed again. "Come on, Viv, let me in." My stomach growled again as I opened the door.

"Don't look at me," I said letting him in. "How did you get here? There is a blizzard outside."

"I live here." He walked into the room.

"You live here?" I asked confused.

"Yep."

"What floor?" How did I not know he lived in the same building I did?

"The top floor."

"The penthouse?" I asked as he pulled out the groceries from the bag. "That's convenient," I said. "What are you doing?"

"Making you lunch, now go put some pants on. You're distracting me," he said eyeing my bare legs.

"Maybe I want to distract you." I said stepping closer to him.

"I know exactly what you want and you can't have it yet." He turned his eyes back to the food he was preparing.

"I'm actually really comfy, I might never put pants on again," I said leaning on the counter.

"Vivie," he warned.

"My house, my rules," I countered.

"My house, my rules," he threw my words back at me.

"What do you mean?" I asked, this was my apartment, although not a lot of my stuff was in it. I didn't actually own any of the furniture or the shiny blue vases that decorated the side tables.

"My company owns this apartment," he said popping a grape into his mouth.

"What?" He repeated himself but I had gone catatonic. "How?"

"Matt called, I offered," he said shrugging. I didn't feel like that was the whole truth. Jack didn't seem like the kind of guy to just offer up things... especially to Matt.

"I need to move." This was too much.

"Wait, what? Why?"

"Because this is weird! You keep paying for things. I'm starting to feel like you're my sugar daddy and not my almost boyfriend," I yelled.

"Don't freak out."

"I'm not freaking out." I yelled. I was freaking out.

"Well it's yours until you graduate whether you use it or not," he said smugly.

"You make everything so complicated." I sighed as I walked into my bedroom to get dressed.

"Baby, you have no idea," he mumbled.

$$$

I convinced Jack to watch *The Notebook* with me. We had lazed around all day snacking on the delicious pasta he had made with chicken and little peas in it. I fell asleep halfway through the movie, but woke when I felt movement. We were no longer sitting. Jack was lying down on the couch and I was cuddled up between his body and the back of the couch. I could see Jack's tear tracks down his face.

"Hey," I said. He wiped his face with his hand. "It's just a movie." I pulled my head from his chest.

"Alzheimer's is an awful disease...I'm going to be making a donation to the cause," he said. I pulled myself closer to him, our faces almost touching.

"You are adorable," I said, kissing him. He kissed back at first, before remembering his game. He mumbled a protest but I slid my body over his, working my hips against his. He stopped protesting and deepened the kiss. Our hands skimmed over each other's bodies, his tongue teased mine as we separated and connected. He moved his hips to meet mine as we rocked back and forth together. I sat up to take off my shirt and his hands rested on my hips, thumbs rubbing against the bones, as he pulled my hips harder against his own. He looked up at me as the pressure continued to build inside of me and I felt like the only girl in the world. Worry flashed through his eyes and I could tell that any minute I was going to lose him. His mouth opened to say something, but I was quicker sliding my tongue into his mouth. I ran the tip over the roof, before kissing him one last time.

"Don't worry Jack," I said a little sad. "You can keep your honor." I climbed off of him and headed toward my bedroom. The way he looked at me had me feeling like one minute I was the queen of the world and then the next I was a piece of garbage on the street. I felt enough guilt about Nick. I felt the guilt on my own; I didn't really need Jack's to accompany it. There were three people I was focusing my anger at. First, Jack, and simply for being Jack. He was confusing, infuriating, and undeniable. I don't think I could say no and leave him behind if I tried. Second, Nick, for being perfect. In the wake of everything that was going on I couldn't name one fault in Nick if I tried. The only thing that was wrong with him was that he wasn't Jack. Third, myself whoever that was now. I was unrecognizable, and I had no idea how to get back to the old me, or if I even wanted to.

I wiped the angry tears from my face. I crawled

into bed and pulled the covers to my eyes. Jack could see himself out. All I had to do was get through the next couple of days and then hopefully this feeling would go away. I heard the knock on the door, I was expecting it. I didn't tell him to come in, I didn't say anything, I just braced myself for the impact. It was his apartment after all and he could do with it what he wanted. Jack stuck his head in as he opened the door. Seeing me in bed he crossed the room in four easy steps and laid on the open space beside me. We laid there silently for what seemed like forever. Jack was staring at the ceiling. I needed to explain, if he wanted the real Genevieve Allen, then he was going to get her.

"I don't want you to fuck me Thursday." I said. He turned to face me scrunching his brows in confusion. "I...I want you to make love to me...now." He closed his eyes pain flashing across his face. "I know you can't and I'm not even sure I could but," I didn't know what to say. The guilt was eating me alive and I knew a part of me wanted to be with Jack to forget about Nick. He opened his eyes and I looked toward the ceiling. "I feel hopeless. What are we doing Jack? We aren't even dating and we're already driving each other insane." I rubbed my eyes, and turned back to him, he looked away...angry.

"I would never ever fuck you. I'm not like that asshole in the bathroom," he said. He had rarely mentioned Molvak before. "I think you are getting scared. I don't think you've ever let anyone love you, because you were too ashamed of your past to love yourself, or for that fact to let anyone into your bubble, but I love you. I love you, Genevieve, and I'm not leaving." He pulled me toward him until I was cradled on his chest. The last thing I heard as I wandered into oblivion was Jack whispering something over and over into my hair.

"Let me love you, Vivie. Let me in."

CHAPTER THIRTY-TWO

I convinced Jack that I was fine Tuesday morning and let him leave for work. He had stayed the whole night. I knew I had overreacted and that everything would be fine after I ended things with Nick. The streets had been mostly cleared by Tuesday night, but Matt insisted I could work from home. He brought over some paperwork and we spent the night eating pizza while he showed me how to do background checks on people. I had told him to take his cut of the money and give the rest back to Jack. He had already paid off my loans a fact that was also starting to rub me the wrong way since we would be officially dating this time Thursday. I didn't know why I couldn't just give it to him. I guess I wanted to separate myself from it as much as possible. In my mind I wanted to forget that we ever had that deal. I kept myself busy Wednesday morning cleaning every surface of my apartment trying not to think about what would happen tonight. I took the EL to the airport worrying my hands together waiting at baggage claim. I saw Nick before he saw me. He looked good, rested, and happy which made my heart hurt more. He spotted me and waved. I waved back and we walked toward each other.

"Miss me?" he asked pulling me into a hug.

"You know it." I said. I really had missed him. If things had gone differently, and Nick and I were just friends, I could have told him about how much of a mind fuck Jack was, but we weren't friends like that and I couldn't tell him anything. We grabbed his bags and headed to the parking lot. The drive was short. I spent the time listening to stories about his dad, nodding at appropriate parts. We pulled up in front of the largest house I had ever seen. The dark brick building stared down at me like it knew I was the enemy. I wondered briefly if it would strike me down before I ever crossed the threshold. Nick shut off the car and turned toward me.

"Don't be nervous. It's just my mom and stepdad," he said squeezing my hand before getting out of the car. I joined him on the steps and we walked together. He rang the bell that echoed through the house. "Breathe, Ginny," he said holding my hand.

Nick's stepdad, John, answered the door. "Welcome!" He was tall with a thick head of gray hair. "You must be, Ginny. We've heard so much about you." He shook my hand moving to let us enter. "Can I get you a drink, Ginny?"

"Water is fine, thank you." I said. He looked at Nick.

"Same, thanks, where's mom?"

"I'm here, I'm here," Grace said "I was finishing setting up the dining room." She embraced Nick. "How's your father? We missed you at Thanksgiving! Your brother disappeared on us too, but he's making up for that tonight." The doorbell rang.

"I've got it." John said handing us two waters and exiting.

"Mom, I would like you to meet Ginny." Nick said.

"It's nice to meet you Ms…" I didn't know what her last name was. Surely it wasn't still Fort.

"Mayburn, dear…I think. There have been so many." She laughed. "It's very nice to meet you too, dear." The handshake she gave me was curt and cold. Yay, this was going to be extra fun. "Oh darling!" Grace said to someone behind me. "I'm so glad this all worked out." I tensed smelling him before seeing him. Grace and Nick all turned to welcome the other member of their family. The other son; the brother that helped Nick out of his mysterious tragic problem, had come home.

"Jack, I want you to meet my girlfriend, Ginny." I turned and stared into the face of the man I loved standing next to the man I was dating. Jack's eyes grew a fraction as he took in who I was. He moved his eyes to Nick and then back to me. I was in big, big trouble. I reached my hand out to shake his.

"Hi, Jack, it's nice to meet you." I said as he wrapped his large hand around mine and squeezed a little too tightly.

"You too… Ginny." Yep, I was definitely in

trouble.

"Everyone hungry?" John asked. Tension filled the room, and I found it hard even to nod my head yes. I let go of Jack's hand as John led us all into the opulent dining room. I lingered behind Grace, John, and Nick.

"This doesn't change anything," I whispered to Jack.

"This changes everything," Jack whispered back, walking into the room. Nick and I sat across from Jack with Grace and John taking the ends of the table. I was physically present for dinner, but mentally I was back in my mom's house reliving the moment Jack told me that he loved me. What did he mean this changes everything? Grace and John asked Nick about his trip while Jack gracefully avoided their questions about what he had done on his holiday break. I listened to every story from Nick again before Jack interrupted the conversation.

"So, Ginny," he said my name like it was acid. "What do you do for a living?" I almost dropped my fork. What was he doing? I set down my utensil before meeting his gaze.

"I'm an administrative assistant," I said knowing full well that what or rather who I was doing for a living was asking me the question.

"Oh really, for what company?" he asked. *For the company of you're an ASS HOLE, JACK!* I thought before answering.

"Not for a company really, my boss promotes..." I paused not knowing what to say. "Things." I said deflated.

"What sort of things?" John chimed in.

"A little bit of everything really, clothing, liquor, jewelry…" I said biting my lip.

"Well that sounds very interesting," Grace said not looking interested at all.

"You don't do anything else?" Jack asked raising his eyebrows.

"She's a student," Nick said.

"Oh that must be very expensive. How are you paying for it?" Jack asked never moving his eyes from mine.

"Jesus, Jack, cool it," Nick said while Grace laughed. I was quickly noticing that Grace laughed at everything, but rarely found anything funny.

"Sorry, Ginny, Jack and I work for a prominent loan company. He never seems to be able to leave work at work." Grace said eyeing Jack and me. Jack glared at me for the rest of dinner, but didn't berate me with questions anymore. I did my best to act the part of a caring girlfriend. I didn't know what Jack was playing at. He surely didn't want me to out us in front of his entire family. Maybe he wasn't playing at all. Jack volunteered to do the dishes although I was positive Grace Mayburn had someone to do that for her. The rest of us moved into the living room where the conversation wasn't interesting enough to pull me out of my head. I had to know what Jack was thinking.

"May I use the restroom?" I asked.

"Of course it's right down the hall across from the kitchen," John said. I didn't need to use the bathroom, I needed to see Jack, to know what he was thinking. I pushed open the swinging door. Jack was standing by the sink. He was wearing bright yellow gloves, but hadn't started washing the dishes yet. His hands were holding onto the edge of a plate as he stared into the soapy water. I grabbed a dish towel ready to dry if any of his family came into the kitchen and saw us.

"Hey," I said startling him.

"Go back to the living room Vivie," he said.

"No, I'm good here," I said. "What's wrong?"

"Are you kidding me?" he whispered. "You're cheating on my brother!"

"Yea with you!" I hissed. Now this was all my fault? "Don't worry in a couple of hours this won't even be an issue," I said.

"Don't do it," he said sadly. "Don't break up with him." I swear the floor fell out from under me and I felt like I was sick. One second he's begging for me to call and break up with Nick and now he doesn't want me at all?

"What… what are you doing?" I grabbed a hold of the sink to steady myself. Jack looked up as we heard the clacking of Graces heels on the hardwood floors.

"Please, Ginny, he can't take it," Jack said picking up a dish. What did that even mean? I didn't get a chance to ask before the door swung open.

"Ginny, are you ok?" Grace asked. "You weren't in the bathroom and I heard talking in here."

"I'm actually not feeling too well," I answered. I needed out of this house and away from sweet clueless Nick, away from delusional Jack, and most definitely away from Grace.

"Nick should take her home," Jack said not

missing a beat.

"Come on dear," Grace said taking my elbow and leading me into the hall. She stopped suddenly turning to face me. "I'm not an idiot, I know something's up between the three of you. I just got my boys back and so help me God if you tear them apart again I will ruin you!" Grace turned from me and continued her quick pace down the hallway. I had no words. The last thing I needed on top of this night was Nick's mom adding fuel to the fire. I followed her into the living room. "Darling, I think you better take Ginny home. She's not feeling too well," Nick stood, a little confused, and we said our goodbyes. John kissed my cheeks and Grace gave me a weak hug.

"What's wrong?" Nick asked.

"Nothing, my stomach. Just take me home," I said pulling out my phone. I gave Nick my address. I couldn't care less if he knew every secret I ever had anymore. If Jack ended things tonight all the worrying and sleepless nights would be for nothing. I wanted Jack and I was willing to do anything to get him.

Meet me tomorrow to talk and I won't break up with him tonight.
– Vivie

I sent the message to Jack as we pulled onto my street.

"You live here?" Nick asked looking up at the tall building. It was a lot nicer than my last apartment. Did he know Jack lived here, too? Sure they were brothers but they were still distant.

"Yes, why?" I asked. He scrunched his brows together. Was he going to ask me? I bit my lip willing him to ask if I had met Jack before tonight, but he didn't.

"Nothing. Want me to walk you up?" he asked.

"No, it's alright. Thanks, Nick." I leaned over and hugged him. I exited the car feeling slow and heavy. My phone beeped at me with a message from Jack.

Deal. – Jack

CHAPTER THIRTY-THREE

I slid my room key into the slot. The green light winked at me as I pushed the door open. The room was dark and empty. I was hoping he would already be here so I couldn't have any more time to think. I knew he was going to throw Nick in my face, obviously. I should have broken it off with him last night so Jack wouldn't be able to use him as ammo. I wondered if his mother had confronted him as well. I was pacing back and forth when I heard his key enter the slot. I ran to the door as it opened and threw myself into him. I kissed him, pouring all of my love into one kiss. He walked me backwards into the room letting the door close behind us.

"Don't leave," I said pulling away. "Just stay. We can fix it." I turned away trying to put some distance in between us, I needed to plead my case. "I know he's Nick and he's your brother and that makes it weird, but that doesn't change the fact that I love you." Before I could continue Jack moved in, kissing my neck. His lips moved down my shoulder and explored the dip of my collar bone. He continued down my arm before running his nose along the side of my torso. Returning to the base of my neck he took a deep breath.

"Stop talking." His lips traveled up my neck. He began nibbling at my ear lobe, sending chills through my body. He wrapped his hands around my waist moving one across my stomach while the other drifted farther south. His strong hands continued their torturing path before he unbuttoned my jeans and slipped his hand inside. I groaned and leaned into him as his curious fingers drew circles on my most sensitive areas.

"Jack, I want you," I said. The pressure building was almost unbearable. He slipped two fingers inside of me. The wave of pleasure increased and I could feel my knees weaken beneath me. The air caught in my lungs as I fought to control my breath.

"I'm right here. Can you feel me?" he breathed into my ear. I could feel him through his pants and I reached back to touch him, mimicking his movements. He removed his hands and let them trail up my body as he slowly began to unbutton my shirt. Letting it fall to the floor. I turned in his arms to look into his eyes. I had no idea what he was thinking. He pulled me closer wrapping his arms around me and kissing me with so much intensity I couldn't think of anything else. He rubbed his hands across my lower back settling them on my behind. Pushing me into him he deepened the kiss until separating and moving to my breasts. He drew them into his mouth one at a time, through the fabric, until I was gasping for air. He teased each nipple before kneeling in front of me. His tongue replace where his hands once were and it was too much. I buckled at the unfamiliar feeling. Jack caught me and stood. For a minute he just held me mumbling incoherently against my neck. He released me and I turned immediately relieving him of his clothes as I kissed my way from his soft lips to his bare chest. He picked me up and laid me on the bed, looking me over before sliding on top of me. I closed my eyes reveling in the feel of his weight on me.

"Open your eyes Viv… Genevieve," he said. I didn't want to miss a second of this moment. Slowly he pushed into me. I felt him fill me. The pleasure building with each teasingly slow movement. I was expecting the pain, but it was bearable, I craved more of him, and tilted my hips toward him urging him to go deeper. He complied and we both became more confident with each thrust. The sound of our synchronized breathing was almost too much to handle.

"Jack," I begged as he increased speed until we couldn't hold on anymore. I burst into a thousand pieces and within seconds Jack joined me. He laid on me breathing heavily before rolling off and pulling me onto his chest.

"I love you, Genevieve," he said kissing my hair. Everything was going to be fine, we were going to work it out. I closed my eyes and let sleep take me.

$$$

The sun woke me, burning through my eyelids. I

felt for Jack but all I found was an envelope. I opened my eyes and sat up. Jack was nowhere to be seen. I got up and walked into the bathroom. He wasn't there; maybe he was getting us breakfast. He wouldn't have left without saying goodbye. I picked up the envelope hoping there was a note inside.

There was... A tiny scrap of paper was wedged in between an insane amount of hundred dollar bills. Confused I turned the paper over.

It's been a pleasure,
Jack Eagle

I turned the paper over in my hands looking for some other message, any kind of loving word written in a corner, but there was nothing. Hot tears pricked my eyes and I quickly wiped them away. I pulled my hair into a pony tail and threw on my clothes.

"You're not getting away that easily." I said, exiting the building. I flagged down a cab outside of the hotel. "Eagle Fort Towers, please," I said to the driver realizing for the first time that Grace had named the building after her sons. As the cab flew down the streets I tried to imagine what Jack was feeling... Guilt? Betrayal? Jealousy? I paid the cabby and ran through the courtyard to the building. "Michael, I need to get up to Jack Eagle's office," I said waiting for him to let me in.

"What's wrong, Ginny? You look like a wreck." He moved around the desk and grabbed my chin lifting it so he could see better.

"Please, Michael, it's an emergency." I begged. "For Matt…" I added hoping that would sway him. I knew lying to Michael was awful but nothing compared to the way I felt when I thought about losing Jack.

"OK, go ahead," he said swiping his card and letting me enter. I ran to the elevator and pushed for the top floor. I blew past the main receptionist and ran straight towards Jack's office. Melissa was sitting at her desk, startled by my sudden entrance.

"Hello, how can I help you?" she asked sweetly.

"Hi, I need to see Ja— Mr. Eagle." I said trying to calm my breathing.

"Do you have an appointment?" she asked sweetly.

"He's expecting me," I said, not entirely a lie, surely he knew me better. "Is he in a meeting?" Interrupting him while he was with a client or colleague wouldn't work in my favor.

"One moment please," she said turning to her phone. "Mr. Eagle, I have a," she paused waiting for my name. She knew my name. Why was she acting like she didn't? Either way I didn't give it to her, I knew that intercom lead straight to his office phone. I wasn't going to give him the option of rejecting me before I even saw him. Hoping he was alone I rushed the door. Melissa never saw it coming and by the time she realized what had happened I was already closing the door. I locked it as she banged on the wood. "I'm calling security!" she yelled. Jack stood up and stared at me before pushing a button on his phone.

"Everything's fine in here Melissa. Sorry for the

theatrics, I can handle this." That stung I wasn't even a person to him anymore I was a thing that he used up and discarded. I was a stray cat that he fed once and then would come back for more, even when the milk had dried up. I wasn't something to love anymore, I was something to handle.

"Hi," I said trying to slow my heart. Between evading Melissa and seeing Jack, my heart was about to beat out of my chest, but I calmed myself. "I mean, good morning," I said straightening.

"What are you doing here, Vivie?" he asked, his face a perfect mask.

"You forgot your giant envelope of money," I said throwing the offending paper on his desk. "People who are in love don't pay for sex."

"You had a job, you did it, you get paid," he said pushing the envelope towards me. I crossed and stood right in front of his desk.

"It wasn't a job, Jack. It hasn't been a job for a while now. I think you know that." I said pushing the envelope back towards him.

"I think you are confused. We had an arrangement. We both followed through and now it's over." The air rushed out of my lungs and my stomach dropped to my feet. I felt the burning tears coming and I didn't know how long I would be able to hold them off.

"You said you loved me." I sobbed. A few tears escaped, and I thought I saw a crack in Jack's perfectly neutral mask. "I love you, I don't know why you're doing this. Is it, is it because of Nick?" I asked. I shouldn't have mentioned Nick because once I did Jack's mask solidified again, stronger than before. I couldn't help the tears now. "You said you loved me," I repeated.

"I said I needed you to trust me, and you did," he said. The world fell away and before I knew what I was doing I had rounded the desk and slapped Jack across the face. He took it, he didn't even try to defend himself or retaliate. I kissed him hard, throwing every emotion behind it and he kissed me back harder. He was saying goodbye, but I was saying see you soon. When we separated Jack stood still, but I bent down tearing a sheet of paper from his printer. I wrote him my own good bye note folded and stuffed it in his coat pocket.

I walked toward the door. "Just because you're throwing yourself under the bus for Nick doesn't mean I am. No matter what, Nick and I end." I turned to look at him one last time. "I don't love him." I opened the door and walked out. I didn't look at Melissa, I didn't look at anyone. Once I got on the elevator I let the tears flow freely. I didn't head out of the building when I hit the lobby. I ran to the one room I knew I could be alone in. I pushed on the door with the sign marked trash. I never felt more like trash than right now. It was locked and I banged hoping someone was inside to let me in.

"Ginny, what the hell? Melissa from Miller Cove call—" Michael paused taking in my appearance. Without another word he swiped his key card and let me in. He didn't follow and I fell in my familiar spot between the two bins.

$$$

I wasn't sure how much time had passed before there was a knock on the door, and then Matt poked his head through.

"I guess it didn't go so well," he said before pulling me to my feet. "We can't be here, Ginny." I knew that I was risking Michael's job. I'm sure the news that some crazy woman had busted into Jack Eagle's office was already trickling down through the floors of the massive building. We went through the back led by Michael. He kept looking from me to Matt and shaking his head. Matt folded me into his car and stopped to talk to his cousin. Their conversation was muffled but it wasn't hard to understand what they were talking about.

"You should have never!" Michael started, but Matt stopped him.

"I know, I messed up…again." He rubbed his hand across his closely shaved head.

"She was a perfectly nice, perfectly normal girl and you… you've… you have broken her. Fix it!" Michael stuttered before turning back into the building. Matt got into the car and pulled out from the building.

"I'll get you home, Ginny. Don't worry everything will be fine," He tried to reassure me.

"Matt, I need you to take me somewhere," I said. He hesitated before answering.

"Where?" he asked.

"Bingo's Bar, I can show you." I gave him the directions. We drove in silence, I knew Matt thought I wanted to drink away my pain and that was fine with me as long as it got me there. This whole mess ended today.

"I don't think they are open," Matt said pulling up to the entrance.

"They aren't, I need to go break up with my boyfriend," I said opening the car door.

"Ginny, are you sure this is the right time?" he asked.

"Positive." I got out of the car and walked the short distance to the bar. I knocked on the door loudly until Ben poked his head out.

"We're clo⁻ Ginny? What the hell happened? Nick!" he yelled inside before hurrying me in. The bar was completely empty.

"What?" Nick yelled popping up from behind the counter. "Ginny?" he asked. Then I walked into the light and he noticed my disheveled appearance, I'm sure I looked like hell. "What the hell happened?" he said jumping over the counter and running to stand in front of me.

"I'm fine Nick I really need to talk to you... in private," I said eyeing Ben, I would miss him terribly if Nick and I didn't get through this. We walked into the back room and Nick closed the door.

"What happened?" he asked again.

"I can't date you anymore, Nick." I said not wanting to waste time or prolong this anymore than I already had.

"What are you talking about?" he asked.

"I'm breaking this off, I can't date you, I can't date anyone," I said. I didn't think I had any tears left to cry.

"Why can't you date anyone?" he asked.

"Because I'm an awful person, I don't even

know who I am anymore."

"I don't accept that," he said. *What does that mean?*

"It's the truth." I said. Why can't he just say ok and be done with it?

"Then we'll work through it together," he said. Why was he always so god damn optimistic?

"I don't think so, Nick, I'm sorry." I squeaked, turning to leave.

"I'm not accepting any of this," he yelled after me. I didn't care if he accepted it or not. I didn't foresee going anywhere but work for the next few weeks. He would get it eventually and move on. I walked past Ben, but before I walked out the door he caught up to me.

"Hey, don't leave; you're part of this family," Ben said. So much for privacy. I couldn't take Ben hating me too, but he would be there for Nick when the time came. "Why are you doing this, Ginny?"

"I'm in love with someone else." Ben's face would haunt me forever. I had betrayed him as much as I had betrayed everyone else. He was right. This was a family, one I had been welcomed into without a second glance, because Nick trusted me, because Nick wanted me. I walked out the door and Ben let me. I dragged my feet on the sidewalk as I walked back to Matt's car. He had been watching me talk to Ben on the threshold.

"Please take me home, Matt," I said buckling myself into his car.

"Ginny, what happened?" Matt asked. "You're giving me another ulcer.

"I'll tell you everything, but right now I can't

because I need to cry." The words were barely out of my mouth before I pulled my legs up to my chest and let the gates open. I felt every emotion from the last four weeks and let them flow out of me. I cried until I was dry. I cried until I was empty.

CHAPTER THIRTY-FOUR

I avoided Nick's phone calls, which were as frequent as breaths in the two weeks since I had broken up with him. Jack had been nonexistent except for the checks he kept sending to my house. I tore up or returned all of them, going as far as to send him half of my pay check every week to pay him back for the money he had already spent on my loans. It kept things tight but I would rather live in squalor than take anything from him. Matt wouldn't let me move back in with him so I was forced to stay in this loft but I accounted for that with the money I was sending Jack to make sure there was enough to count as rent. He hadn't cashed a single check and I was sure he was treating them with the same respect I was treating his.

In all the chaos that my life had churned up, there was one constant always in the back of my mind. I needed money, and if I was going to move out of the apartment that did nothing but remind me of Jack, I was going to need more of it. I had asked Matt if he had any johns that I could go to, but he refused. There was no way he was going to let me anywhere near that side of the business again. I had no choice; I had to go to the one person who wanted me. The one person who could afford to have me.

I walked down the familiar hall of the Motor Bay Motel where I had agreed to meet him. I checked in at reception and the man at the desk handed me my payment. Matt had used this motel when he first started working with the girls, and although it had been many years since they had used a dump like this, the receptionist knew the rules. The john handed the payment over to the clerk, who passed it on to the girls, taking his cut of course. I stashed the cash in my car then I reentered the motel. This place was beyond dingy. The cigarette smoke had seeped into the wall paper turning it yellow. I found room 69 cringing, he had probably asked for that room specifically. Before I knocked I pulled out my phone, I knew I was being reckless and stupid, but I wasn't an idiot I needed to tell someone where I was.

**Matt, If you don't hear from me
in an hour, call 911 and send them
to Motor Bay Motel. Room 69
– Ginny**

I pressed send and knocked on the door before turning my phone on silent. The door opened and I shook as I looked at the disgusting man standing before me.

"Hello, doll," Jeremy Molvak said opening the door wider.

"You have thirty minutes," I said walking in. He had a selection of toys laid out on the bed. "Those aren't part of our deal, Jeremy," I said picking up a bottle of lube.

"I know. I thought you might change your mind," he said.

"I didn't. Get rid of them." He picked up the toys and shoved them in a backpack that was leaning against the bed. He held out his hand for the lube.

"No, I'll need this." I said. Knowing there was no way Molvak was going to get me wet where it counted.

"I forgot how feisty you were," he said laughing.

"So what did you have in mind?" I asked him wanting to sit but not trusting any service. I sat reluctantly realizing soon it wouldn't matter.

"I want to watch you watch porn, and I want you to beat me off while you do it, and then I'm going to bend you over and ride you till you cum all over my cock," Jeremy said leaning in close. "How does that sound?" he asked. I shrugged, what did he want from me? I was here and I was willing.

"Whatever, no kissing," I said while he smiled.

"Then let's get started."

He inserted a cd into the laptop he had set up on the bed. The mattress groaned under his weight as he shifted next to me. He was silent as he pressed play. I thought Jeremy Molvak was disgusting before, but after watching the first five minutes of his porn I was revolted. Jeremy was into violent, dark things. I closed my eyes.

"Eyes open," he said as he undid his pants. He reached over and grabbed my hand, holding it up to my mouth. "Spit," he said. Cringing I pooled the saliva in my mouth and spit it into my hand. Keeping my eyes on the screen I let Molvak lead my hand down and around his shaft. He moved it up and down never letting go increasing and decreasing the pressure as he pleased himself with my hand. I looked at the clock fifteen minutes had gone by and I knew what was coming next. "Take off your clothes," Jeremy said releasing his hand from mine. I stripped off my dress, the same red velvet one I had worn the first time I'd met Jeremy. I unsnapped my bra and shimmied out of my panties. "Lay on your stomach," he ordered staring at my naked body. I laid down and closed my eyes. I could hear Jeremy undressing and felt how the bed dipped as he climbed on it. He rubbed his hands over my backside caressing the curves. When he was ready he spread my legs and knelt in between them. I was breathing heavily now, not from excitement but from fear. I heard the doorknob turn as someone entered. I turned my head to see who was coming in, scared Jeremy had thought to make this some sort of gang bang revenge for what Jack had done to him.

"This room is occupied for another ten minutes!" Jeremy yelled.

"Back the fuck off of her!" Jack yelled as he pushed past the same receptionist I had gotten my payment from. Jeremy recognized Jack and immediately backed off. "Get up, Ginny, get dressed."

"What are you doing here?" I said covering myself.

"Get your clothes and wait for me in the fucking hallway!" Jack yelled at me.

"Hey, I already paid her!" Jeremy yelled from the corner he was cowering in.

"Jack, this is none of your business get out!" I yelled. "Jeremy let's finish this!" I laid back down on the bed. Jack's face was the color of a tomato as he threw a wad of cash at Jeremy hitting him in his protruding gut, and bent down wrapping the comforter around me like I was a burrito and lifting me over his shoulder.

"Jack put me down!" I screamed, as he grabbed my purse and carried me out of the room. "What about my clothes?" I screamed.

"You won't need that dress anymore," Jack said walking down through the lobby. People stopped and stared as we passed and I tried to hide my face.

"Jack, this is embarrassing," I said kicking my feet. He didn't stop he didn't even pause as I kicked and hit at him. I saw Henry standing by the car. "NO, Jack I can drive myself home." Henry opened the passenger door and Jack threw me in the front seat. He turned toward Henry with my bag while blocking me from trying to escape. Henry handed him the keys to the car.

"Don't leave this spot until I get in and start driving." He handed Henry my bag and walked to the driver's side sliding in next to me. He started the engine and sped off, I could make out Henry walking in the direction of my car.

"What the fuck do you think you're doing?" I

asked as we pulled on the highway. Jack reached into the backseat and pulled a t-shirt from a duffle bag. He threw it at me and I quickly slipped it on. It smelled like him, and I momentarily forgot how upset I was as I inhaled the scent I missed so much.

"What the fuck am I doing? What the fuck were you doing? With that guy! Of all the men in the world you pick that guy!" he yelled at me.

"How did you know I was with him?" I asked curious. Obviously Matt had called him when he had gotten my text.

"I didn't!" he ran his hand through his hair. "In fact I still can't believe it was actually that guy! Are you insane?"

"Matt wouldn't give me any johns..." I said as an explanation.

"No shit, he wouldn't give you any men, I told him if he did I would walk and he'd be fucked for clients, money, clothes everything. I would drag his name through the mud and every girl that decided to continue working for him."

"Who the hell do you think you are?" I said. "I still don't get why you are here! You've made it pretty clear you couldn't give a shit about me. I break up with Nick and still nothing, I know he told you so don't even act surprised," I said remembering how a small part of me held on to the thought that maybe he would come back to me, but he didn't.

"I still don't understand why you're even thinking about sleeping around," he shouted.

"ARE YOU KIDDING ME?" I yelled beyond furious. "I need the money, Jack. I swear I don't understand how you don't get that people need money to buy things. We aren't all born rich."

"YOU HAVE MONEY!" he said equally as angry. "I will give you anything you need, you wanted your loans gone, I made them go away, you wanted a house, I gave you a house, I gave you a giant pile of money, and you still need more! Money isn't everything, Vivie!"

"It is when you don't have any!" I said.

"I just told you that I—" he said

"I don't want your money, Jack!" I yelled. He was never going to get it. I couldn't take his money because I didn't want to rely on him, I trusted him once and it didn't turn out so well. Also I needed to be self-sufficient. I needed to make my own way in the world.

"Why?" he asked.

"I don't want you!" I screamed. It wasn't true. If he had asked me to take him back right now, I would in a heartbeat. He starred out the window his perfect jaw set tight.

"Then you should be with Nick," he said with a tone of finality.

"Don't start with that stuff again, Jack, really, it's old."

"Do you know why I couldn't take you away from him? It's not like it even matters now. Once a monster always a monster right, Vivie?" he asked.

"Don't even try to play that card here, Jack. I know your game. Nick told me all about it. You save people and then disappear. You make yourself a constant source in someone's life and then you run away." Jack turned to look at me. That had done it. Whatever love he might have felt was gone now as he looked at me with pure hatred.

"Nick got addicted to meth in high school. That's why Grace made him move up here. But you know Nick, he's a friendly guy and made some real shitty friends from the start. He ran away and..." he stopped. "I found him eventually almost dead living on the street. I cleaned him up, got him in rehab. You're the first girl he's dated since getting clean," he finished. That was the big trouble Nick was talking about. I felt like an idiot for not asking him about it these last couple weeks.

"He hasn't relapsed," I said not sure if it was a question or a statement, because he had been calling me. I felt for Jack and Nick and even Grace a little bit, but it didn't change anything. We all had pasts to deal with. We turned into the building's drive, and Jack got out. He crossed the car and opened the door. I wrapped the comforter around my hips since I still didn't have pants on.

"No, he hasn't," Jack said. Henry appeared with my car and entered the garage. I wasn't surprised that he knew which spot was mine. He would be back shortly to get Jack's car. "That's why we– that's why nothing can ever happen, that's why he can't ever know," Jack said.

I thought I would be relieved when I found out why, but the sadness encased me again and I wanted to run and hide, pretend there was still hope, but there wasn't.

"This is goodbye isn't it?" I asked. He nodded. I stepped closer to him and he let me kiss him one last time.

CHAPTER THIRTY-FIVE

It had been thirty days since I had seen Jack. I wish I could say that it had gotten easier, but it hadn't. I missed him so much. Matt finally got fed up with my moping around the office and offered me a job as a brand ambassador for Black Tie Vodka. I still worked my regular office hours with him, but at night I would hit up some of the most exclusive clubs in the city to promote the drink. I think he thought it would take my mind off of Jack, but wherever I went he seemed to pop up. Not ever physically, but the men who enjoyed the overpriced vodka, along with the women who provided it, mentioned him often.

"So you work for Jack?" Mr. Bergman said one night.

"No, I work for Matt." I said pouring him another shot.

"Same difference," he said.

"Not really... I don't work on that side of the

business," I said as his eyes roamed over my body.

"Really? I thought all the girls did," he said.

"Nope, Mr. Eagle doesn't want me working for that side of things," I said. I wasn't bitter anymore. This new job gave me enough additional income to not freak out or have to worry about living in my car again. Mr. Bergman laughed.

"He's always been a selfish son of a bitch," he said.

"Oh, so you've met Grace." I laughed, thinking about Jack's mother. One of the many reasons it would never work out between us. Those reasons didn't matter to me though. I knew I would always want Jack no matter what got in our way. A part of me hated that... another reminder that I am my mother's daughter. Bergman laughed louder.

"Met her? Hell, I married her once!" he said. I let my mouth open in shock a tiny bit before realizing I was being rude.

"Jack's not selfish though, not really. He's stubborn," I said.

"Yea, he's a tough cookie to crack." He rubbed his chin with his free hand. "Ms.?"

"Ginny." I said putting the top back on the bottle.

"Ginny, I'm throwing a party tomorrow night with a bunch of crotchety old men." He paused to take another drink. "Grouchy, boring men who would drop a lot of money on liquor... Would you be interested in coming? I mean, of course, serving as a hostess while selling your fine vodka. No funny business either. I swear just old men playing poker," he assured me.

"Well I'd have to check with Matt," I said. Mr.

Bergman handed me his card with his address and number on it.

"Matt will say yes. Be there at seven tomorrow night," he said, downing the rest of his drink.

"Thanks Mr. Bergman," I replied pouring him more.

"Larry," he said. "Call me Larry."

$$$

Larry was right.

"Larry Bergman!?!" Matt yelled. "I've been trying to get into his private parties for years!"

"Yea, well he wants me there tonight at seven. He's safe right?" I asked. The last thing I needed was more drama.

"Yea. He was one of our first clients, but he quit coming, if ya know what I mean," he said.

"Little blue pills?" I asked confused.

"No, he got married," he said. I laughed. So many of our clients were married. "Yea, I know. He actually loved her though," Matt said. "Take three cases tonight and give the clients a bottle to take home with them." Wow! Matt giving away free booze? He must really want me to keep getting invited to these parties.

"Wanna come?" I asked. Why couldn't Matt come? I'm sure Larry wouldn't mind.

"No, I can't impose like that," he said smiling a little. He really wanted to, but didn't want to jeopardize the fragile relationship.

"What if you just come help me set up? Say hi to Mr. Bergman and then excuse yourself," I suggested. His smile grew bigger as he considered this.

"Well, you will need some help carrying all those cases," he said.

$$$

"Ginny!" Mr. Bergman said welcoming me into his condo. It was a few blocks away from mine. "Who is that behind you?" he asked.

"You remember Matt, Larry." I said. "I couldn't carry the cases by myself so I asked him to help."

"Matt! Of course, you look different," he said shaking Matt's free hand. "Why so many cases?" he asked. We settled on five not knowing how many people were coming.

"What kind of hostess would I be if I didn't bring favors?" I said. Larry eyed me coolly. He wasn't a dumb man. He knew that Matt wanted to be included in his parties, and he knew I was Matt's ticket in. I just didn't know if Larry liked me enough to let me get away with it.

"Matt, why don't you stay for the game," he said. I gave Larry my biggest smile, and he winked at me.

"Thank you, Mr. Bergman," he said. Larry didn't give Matt the benefit of calling him Larry.

Once the bottles were open and the guests started to arrive I fell into my role easily. Larry answered the door for the first guest.

"Craig! You stupid piece of shit, get in here. This is Ginny," he said.

"Nice to meet you," he said as I took his coat.

"You too," I replied.

"Ginny, if you wouldn't mind taking Craig's coat into the guest room and then meet us in the game room, please."

Once the coat was hung I went into the game room where Craig and Matt had been introduced. I poured them all a large glass of Black Tie Vodka. Fifteen minutes later most of the guests had trickled in. My routine was simple; I answered the door, showed them to the game room, and hung their coats. I smiled at Larry who was doing a good job of including Matt. The men told stories about their past shenanigans. I understood why it was so hard to get into this group now; they had been friends for decades.

"Why haven't you boys started?" I asked looking at the untouched poker table while I refilled their drinks.

"Waiting on Larry's boy to show." Craig said. On cue the doorbell rang. I walked into the foyer plastering a smile on my face. Opening the door I laughed. There he was—the one person I wouldn't dare to expect. What was he doing here? I was just beginning to get used to the idea of never seeing him again. Jack stood staring; perplexed.

"Hello, Mr. Eagle." I said forcing my smile bigger. It still hurt to look at him, and not be able to touch him. "May I take your jacket?" I finished. He looked like he had just come from work. His long black coat covered his sharp black suit. He was still in shock, his mouth slightly open. I wanted to kiss it. To forget all the outside circumstances that kept us apart, but I couldn't. I was helpless to the situation; hopeless. All I could do was clamp my teeth together and keep smiling.

"What are you doing here?" he asked in a rushed whisper. My smile fell a little. I knew he loved me. In my bones I felt it, but when he spoke to me like that, with no warmth, I felt like it was all a dream. *It's been a pleasure.* His note to me after the only time we had truly been together flashed in my head. Maybe it had all just been in my head.

"Nice to see you, too," I said icily. "Your coat?" I asked holding out my hand. He slipped out of his jacket and his suit coat, handing them both to me. His face was still a mass of confusion. "The game room is that way," I said pointing him in the right direction.

"I know where the fucking game room is, Vivie. The question is why do you?" he continued in a whisper.

"Your dad—" I started.

"Stepdad," he corrected.

"Your stepdad is my new client." I paused genuinely smiling now at the look of horror on his face. "And don't call me Vivie," I said walking into the room being used as a coat closet. A part of me wanted him to follow. I wanted to scream and yell at him. I wanted us to scream and yell at each other, because then I'd at least get to be near him, get to smell him. I missed talking to him, even if all we ever did was piss each other off. I knew saying his stepdad was my new client was wrong, and catty, but all I wanted was him. Even though I knew why he did it, I still hated the way he ended things. I wanted to tell him how much I wanted him, but whenever I opened my mouth the only things that came out were words meant to hurt him, just like he hurt me. I threw his jacket on the chair and watched it slide off and fall to the floor. Shaking it out I placed it gently on the back of the chair. Smoothing out my dress I noticed a piece of paper on the rug. It must have fallen out of one of the jackets. I picked it up unfolding the worn paper. My breath caught in my throat.

Jack,
It could always be, just you and me.
I love you.
Genevieve

The note I had given him the morning after our third date. It was so worn he must have read it a hundred times. I held the note in my hand walking into the game room. The boys had started to play and were passing around multiple bottles of the expensive vodka. Matt and Larry looked up at me, simultaneously winking. I smiled at them knowing they would be fast friends. I could only see half of Jack's face. He didn't look phased at all. I laughed realizing it was Thursday. I knew it was just another night to him, but to me it felt like I was missing out on something tonight. Less than a month ago we would be laughing, or yelling, or drinking together. I didn't think we would ever be the same people again. I looked at his sharp features. The way his bold eyes darted back and forth sizing up his opponents. I turned away as my eyes watered. Jack had wanted my trust and I had given it to him.

Although I was positive I would always love him, I didn't know if I could ever trust him again.

$$\$\$\$$$

"Here's your payment, Honey," Larry said handing me a check. "I want you here every Thursday," he said. "You too, Matt." Matt couldn't hide his smile. I took the check staring at it.

"Whoa Larry, this is too much," I said.

"No it's not. It's the perfect amount," he said relying on the wall a little too much.

"Ok, but I'll wait to cash it until you're sober," I said laughing. Larry cocked one of his bushy eyebrows at me.

"Good girl," he said pulling me in for a hug.

Matt and I left together. He wasn't drunk, but he was high on the feeling of being accepted. He skipped down the steps of the building.

"Ginny, oh my God, you're magic! That was amazing! Now Jack can really go fu—" he stopped as Jack rounded the corner.

"Genevieve, can I talk to you?" he said. I was startled. I still had my note to him in my pocket.

"Can you give us a second?" I asked Matt. I had filled him in on everything that had happened after the scene at the motel.

"Sure," he said giving Jack a dirty look. He only took a few steps back not trusting Jack enough to go any farther.

"Yes?" I said sticking my hands in my pockets and running my finger along the edge of the note.

"What was that tonight?" he asked. Did he really

think I was going to sleep with Larry?

"Us common folk call it working," I said my tone dripping with bitterness.

"Why Larry?" he asked. I shrugged. I liked Larry. He was nice and honest.

"He offered and I was available," I said "He hates your mother more than I do so I figured he must be an ok guy."

"Viv—Genevieve, don't be nasty," he said. The silence stretched.

"Is that it? You just wanted to make sure I wasn't fucking your dad?" I said rumpling the note in my pocket. *Tell me you still love me.* I thought. *Tell me anything to make it better.*

"No, I mean..." he paused running his hands through his hair. "How are you?"

I sighed. What did he want from me? He didn't want to see me; he did want to see me. Which was it? Love or Hate? Or worse neither; was he completely indifferent to me?

"I've been swell! I'm living in this really nice apartment that I got from this really attractive asshole that broke my heart...you?" I spit the words at him watching them cut him down.

"Genevieve—" he started.

"Don't Jack! I guess I was right. It could've been just you and me, if you would stop bringing other people into it," I said sadly. "I'm not sure why I keep holding onto that."

Jack fumbled in his pockets; they were empty.

"You went through my coat?" he asked

"No it fell out," I said. Jeeze, I was a wannabe prostitute not a thief. "Why are you carrying it around anyway?" I asked. I had to know.

"You know why," he said. Why did he always assume that I knew things I didn't? It was infuriating!

"I don't know much of anything anymore," I replied dully.

"You know," he said again. He looked so vulnerable. I shrugged. "Do you really want me to say it even though it won't change anything?" he yelled. Matt shifted behind me. "Fine! I love you! Does that make it better for you? If I could turn away from everything, I would. If it only affected you and me I would quit my job and start all over with you, but I can't."

"That's not it," I said angrily.

"Oh really?" he said stepping closer. "What is it then?"

"You don't trust. You don't trust Nick to stay sober, you don't trust me to stand by you when you have nothing, and you don't trust yourself. You don't trust your heart so you run away!" I yelled hot tears brimming in my eyes.

"You don't know that. You weren't there with Nick the last time," he whispered completely ignoring my other arguments.

"Jack he's—" I started.

"YOU DON'T KNOW!" he yelled. Matt stepped in front of me.

"Step back, Jack," he said, his voice eerily calm. "If you want her, she's right here; crazy in love with you, but if you don't, then leave it. Leave her alone."

"I'm trying..." Jack said tears coming to his

eyes. For the first time I realized how worried Jack was about Nick. I had to let him go; to let them both go. I stepped around Matt. The note in hand. I reached out to Jack squeezing the square of paper back into his hand.

"It could never be you and me. Bye Jack." I said turning back to Matt. We left and sat in the car silently while I calmed down enough to drive us home.

$$$

I laid in my bed. I moved to my couch. Nowhere felt comfortable. Nowhere felt safe. I texted Matt a few times knowing his phone was probably turned off and he was asleep. I tried to stop thinking about Jack. I was right from the beginning; he was the wrong choice. If it even was a choice. I thought of the things I needed to do tomorrow. I should catch up with Michael and Robin, I thought. Our friendships were new and I was already ruining them. My phone rang and I smiled knowing it was probably Matt calling to tell me to stop texting him. The ringing was probably driving him crazy.

"I know, Matt, I'm sorry I'll stop." I said.

"Ginny?" Nick said. Why was Nick calling me now? We hadn't spoken in weeks.

"Nick?" I asked shocked. Why? Why didn't I look at the caller ID? "How are you?" I asked not sure what else I should say.

"Is it true?" he asked. Oh no. Did he find out? How did he find out? No, no he couldn't have. It had to be something else. "Is it true? You and

Jack?" he clarified. *Oh shit, oh shit!* I thought. That secret was in the vault; how did he find out? The doorbell rang. I walked over to it not answering Nick because I simply didn't know what to say.

"Jack?" I asked opening the door. "What are you doing here?" Nick was in my ear again before he could answer. I held up my finger for him to wait.

"Do you love him?" Nick asked. It wasn't a hard answer. After everything that had happened I still loved Jack. I would always love Jack.

"Yes." I whispered. "I'm sorr—" I started.

"Bye, Ginny," he said as the line went dead. I pulled the phone away from my ear and stared at it. Panic flowed through me. Goodbye? What does that mean? Goodbye like I never want to see you again? Or goodbye like I'll never see you again?

"Is Nick here?" Jack asked.

"How did he know?" I said looking at him.

"Was that him?" he pointed at the phone. "Where is he?"

"Did you tell him?" I asked.

"He found the note." Jack said running his hands through his hair. I started to shake. I loved Nick, just not in the way that I loved Jack. I never wanted him to get hurt; I never wanted anything bad to happen although it was always inevitable. Jack was right, he should have never known.

"He said goodbye…" I said staring at the phone again. "What does that mean, Jack?

"Get your coat," Jack said dialing some numbers on his phone. I looked at the phone in my hand and back to Jack.

"Where are we going?" I asked afraid of the

answer. This could have all been avoided. Why couldn't I love Nick? Why did Jack have to come into my life? Nick wouldn't do anything dangerous or stupid would he? The snow had started to fall again. In a matter of hours the streets would be abandoned as people sought shelter. Where could he be?

"We're going to find him." Jack said taking my hand in his.

End

Saving Myself

CONNECT WITH ME

Facebook:
http://facebook.com/AndreaBlackWrites

http://facebook.com/SavingMyself